Edmund Waller

Poetical Works Of Edmond Waller

Vol. I.

Edmund Waller

Poetical Works Of Edmond Waller
Vol. I.

ISBN/EAN: 9783337103439

Printed in Europe, USA, Canada, Australia, Japan

Cover: Foto ©Andreas Hilbeck / pixelio.de

More available books at **www.hansebooks.com**

EDMUND WALLER Efq.

Robert Edgdon's Potteries Land Chryftalfabes Collection. *grav. fc.*

Printed for John Bell near Exeter Exchange Strand London Nov.th 1777.

BELL'S EDITION.

The POETS of GREAT BRITAIN

COMPLETE FROM

CHAUCER to CHURCHILL.

WALLER VOLUME I.

He catch'd at Love, and fill'd his arms with Bays.

Printed for John Bell near Exeter Exchange Strand London Nov. 1ˢᵗ 1777.

THE
POETICAL WORKS
OF
EDMUND WALLER.

IN TWO VOLUMES.

FROM MR. FENTON'S QUARTO EDIT. 1729.

WITH

THE LIFE OF THE AUTHOR.

When WALLER, kindling with celestial rage,
View'd the bright Harley of that wond'ring age,
His pleasing pain he taught the lute to breathe;
The Graces sung, and wove his myrtle wreath----
His Muse, by Nature form'd to please the fair,
Or sing of heroes with majestic air,
To melting strains attun'd her voice, and strove
To waken all the tender powers of love----
The florid and sublime, the grave and gay,
From WALLER's beams imbibe a purer ray----
Maker and model of melodious verse!
Accept these votive honours at thy herse.   FENTON.

VOL. I.

EDINBURG:
AT THE Apollo Press, BY THE MARTINS.
Anno 1777.

THE

POETICAL WORKS

OF

EDMUND WALLER.

VOL. I.

CONTAINING HIS

MISCELLANIES.

Tho' poets may of infpiration boaft,
Their rage, ill-govern'd, in the clouds is loft.
He that proportion'd wonders can difclofe,
At once his fancy and his judgment fhows.
Chafte moral writing we may learn from hence,
Neglect of which no wit can recompenfe.....
Well-founding verfes are the charm we ufe,
Heroic thoughts and virtue to infufe.
Things of deep fenfe we may in profe unfold,
But they move more in lofty numbers told :---
For rudeft minds with harmony were caught,
And civil life was by the Mufes taught.
POEM TO LORD ROSCOMMON.

EDINBURG:
AT THE Apollo Prefs, BY THE MARTINS.
Anno 1777.

EDMUND WALLER.

It has been frequently obferved, that the life of a poet affords but few materials for a narrative, and that the time of his birth and death, with the intervening dates of his publications, are the chief anecdotes of him which we can tranfmit to pofterity. This opinion has been the lefs controverted, becaufe long received : but however infignificant the life of a poet may be thought in itfelf, or however difficult it may be to trace his progrefs through it, the life of Waller, it is hoped, will afford many interefting particulars to the generality of readers.

Edmund Waller was born on the 3d of March 1605, at Colefhill, in the county of Hertford. He was the fon of Robert Waller, Efq. of Agmondefham in Buckinghamfhire, by Anne, the fifter of John Hampden, Efq. the celebrated republican who diftinguifhed himfelf fo much in the beginning of the Civil wars, and who was killed at the battle of Chalgrove.

Robert, our Poet's father, was bred to the profeffion of the law; but exchanging that ftudy for a country retirement, by economy, and application to agriculture, he improved his paternal fortune; and dying whilft our Author was in a ftate of infancy, left him heir to 3500 *l.* a-year.

The care of young Waller's education now devol-

ved on his mother. He was fent to Eton fchool, and
to King's College in Cambridge; but Mr. Wood, in
his *Athen. Oxon.* fays, that he was moftly trained in
grammar learning under Mr. Dobfon, minifter of
Great Wycombe in Bucks. He gave early difcoveries
of that acutenefs of imagination which afterwards
breathed through his poetical and profe compofitions;
for at fixteen years of age he was elected burgefs for
Aymefham, and took his feat in the Houfe of Commons in the third parliament of James I. That our
Author did not exceed the years heve afcribed to him,
is evident from his own words ; "I was but fixteen,"
fays he, "when I fat firft; and fometimes it has
" been thought fit that young men may be early in
" councils, that they may be alive when others are
" dead." And hence Lord Clarendon has obferved,
in his character of young Waller, "that he was nurfed
" in parliaments." He obtained a feat in parliament
a fecond time, before arriving at the age of manhood,
for the borough of Chipping-Wycombe in Buckinghamfhire, in the firft parliament of Charles I.; and
in the third parliament of the fame prince he was
again elected for Aymefham.

  Our Author began to give proofs of his poetical
genius fo early as the year 1623, when he had not
exceeded his 18th year, as appears from the copy
of verfes "Upon the danger his Majefty (being prince)
" efcaped in the road of St. Andero ;" for there

Prince Charles, before setting sail for England, after long soliciting a marriage with the Infanta at the Spanish court, gave a magnificent entertainment on board the British admiral, then in the port of St. Andero, to some Spanish noblemen who had escorted him from Madrid; but in going a-shore, the prince, with his company, were on the point of perishing in a violent storm. In this beautiful panegyric we meet with that unexpected, yet natural approximation, comparison, and contrast of different images, which characterize the writings of Waller. Yet, perhaps, it was not so much owing to his wit, his fine parts, or his **talent** for poetry, that he came first to be publicly known and distinguished, as to his carrying off the daughter and sole heirefs of a rich citizen, against a rival whose interest was espoused by the court. This lady was Anne, the daughter of Richard Banks, Esq. and Waller's rival was a gentleman of the name of Crofts, who paid his addrefses to the lady backed by the influence and interest of the court. It is not known at what time he married this lady, but he was a widower before reaching his 25th year, when he began to entertain a passion for Sachariffa, which was a fictitious name for the Lady Dorothy Sidney, the eldest daughter of the Earl of Leicester, afterwards Countess of Sunderland. She was one of the celebrated beauties of that age, and in her were united every personal and mental accomplishment.

He now lived more expenfively than ufual, was known at court, was careffed by all the people of quality who had any relifh for wit and polite literature, and made one of that celebrated club of which Lord Falkland, Mr. Chillingworth, Sir Francis Wenman, Mr. Godolphin, and other diftinguifhed men, were members. By mixing with the learned and virtuous, our ideas are arranged, our knowledge becomes more diffufed, and our beft habits are formed and ftrengthened; for the clofet only begins that work which fociety completes, by giving the mind all that embellifhment and dignity which it is capable of receiving.

At one of thefe meetings this illuftrious club of wits heard a noife in the ftreet, and were told that a fon of Ben Johnfon was arrefted. The unhappy man was fent for, who proved to be Mr. George Morley; afterwards Bifhop of Winchefter. Mr. Waller liked him fo well that he paid the debt, which was about 100 l. on condition he agreed to live with him at Beaconsfield. Mr. Morley did fo for feveral years; and Waller ufed frequently to acknowledge, that from this gentleman he imbibed a tafte for the ancient writers, and acquired what he had of their manner. As Mr. Waller, prior to this incident with Morley, had given fpecimens of his poetical genius, we are only to fuppofe that Morley improved and refined this propenfity.

The above circumstance is contradicted by Lord Clarendon, and, upon his authority, by Mr. Stockdale, who has lately obliged the world with the life of our Poet. According to this last biographer, Morley, who was one of the politest scholars of the age, was related to our Author, and their love of letters produced an intimacy and friendship between them. He further observes, " that Morley used often to visit Waller at " Beaconsfield, and assist him in his literary progress. " He directed him in his choice of books; he read " with him the capital authors of antiquity; he en- " larged his understanding, and refined his taste. " That his cousin Waller, therefore, might gain all " possible improvement, and rise to that consequence " which he might derive from his uncommon abi- " lities, he introduced him into Lord Falkland's " club."——" He brought him," says Lord Clarendon, " into that company which was most celebrated for " good conversation."

During the long intermission of parliaments, from 1629 to 1640, Waller dedicated most of his time to the prosecution of his studies. At length a parliament was called in the 1640, which is called the Short Parliament, as it met on the 13th of April, and was dissolved before the end of May. This long recess of parliament having disgusted the nation, and raised jealousies against the designs of the court, which would be sure to discover themselves whenever the King came to ask a supply, Mr. Waller, elected for Aymesham, resolved to attack the late measures of the court, and plead the cause of freedom and the people. On the 22d April 1640, in a most animated speech, fortunately preserved, he gives us some notions of his general principles in government. He proposed to the House, that the necessary subsidies should be granted to the King, but that before they were taken into consideration the faults of administration should be examined and redressed, liberty confirmed, and property secured. This speech does Waller honour, as it evinces he was equally an enemy to despotism and anarchy, and that he meant not to abridge the lawful authority of the King, though he strenuously vindicated the rights of the people.

The Long Parliament met on the 3d of Nov. 1640, in which Waller again represented Aymesham for the third time. Being now warmly actuated with that general spirit of opposition to the court, which the abrupt dissolution of the preceding parliament, and other unpopular measures of the King and his ministers had excited, (although it does not appear that at this crisis he harboured any rebellious designs against his sovereign) Waller was appointed to support the impeachment against Judge Crawley. Accordingly, on the 16th July 1641, at a conference of the Two Houses, he delivered the impeachment, and enforced it with a speech replete with pointed wit and nervous eloquence; a speech so highly applauded, that 20,000 copies of it were sold in one day. Yet did it not effect its purpose, as no punishment was inflicted on Crawley, a Justice of the Court of Common Pleas, and one of the twelve Judges, and whose crime was that of subscribing to an opinion that the King had a right to levy ship-money.

Matters having now come to an extremity betwixt the King and his parliament, Charles, on the 22d of August 1642, erected the royal standard at Nottingham, and on this occasion our Author sent his Majesty a thousand broad pieces; a pretty convincing proof that he wished not ill to the royal cause; at the same time corresponding with those more immediately employed about the King's person; by their means he obtained the royal leave for returning to his duty in parliament, where it was expected he would be of singular service to his prince by the force of his eloquence.

Soon after the battle of Edge-hill, which was fought on the 23d Oct. 1642, Charles retired to Oxford, where Waller was one of the Commissioners appointed by the parliament to present their propositions of peace. The Commissioners were received by his Majesty in the garden of Christ-Church, and Waller, as the lowest in rank, was presented last. After having kissed the royal hand, Charles looking on him with complacency, said, "Though you are the last,

" yet you are not the worst, nor the least in my fa-
" vour."

As Whitelocke, who was also one of the Commiffioners deputed by the parliament gives testimony to
the above anecdote, we can hardly question its authen-
ticity; and though that author's veracity ought not to
be disputed in narrating a fact of which himself was
witness, yet ought we not wholly to rely on the conclufions which he deduces from it. He more than
once afferts, that the favourable reception conferred
upon Waller by the King at Oxford was in confe-
quence of the plot then forming by him for his Majefty's interest, and which was detected in a short
time after the return of the Commiffioners to London. But it is hardly probable that Charles should
commit a folecifm in politics fo extremely flagrant,
if he really knew that Waller had affociated against
his foes, as thus to take public and particular notice
of him on that account, and confequently mark him
a victim of the parliament's wrath, should his concert
mifcarry.

This plot was formed and difcovered in the 1643,
and was of fo mild a nature, that Mr. Hume fays, "it
" might with more justice be styled a project than a
" plot." Mr. Whitelocke has given the following account of this affair *.

· " June 1643," fays he, "began the arraignment of

* Memorials of Englifh affairs, p. 70. edit. 1732.

" Waller, Tomkins, Challoner, and others, confpi-
" ring to furprife the City militia, and fome members
" of parliament, and to let in the King's forces to
" furprife the City, and diffolve the parliament. Wal-
" ler, a very ingenious man, was the principal actor
" and contriver of this plot, which was in defign
" when he and the other Commiffioners were at Ox-
" ford with the parliament's propofitions, and that
" being then known to the King, occafioned him to
" fpeak thefe words to Waller, *Though you are the laft,*
" *yet you are not the worft, nor the leaft in favour.* When
" he was examined touching this plot, he was afked
" whether Selden, Pierpoint, Whitelocke, and others
" by name, were acquainted with it? He anfwered,
" That they were not; but that he did come one
" evening to Selden's ftudy, where Pierpoint and
" Whitelocke then were with Selden, on purpofe to
" impart it to them all; and fpeaking of fuch a
" thing in general terms, thefe gentlemen did fo in-
" veigh againft any fuch thing as treachery and bafe-
" nefs, and that which might be the occafion of fhed-
" ding much blood, that he faid he durft not, for the
" awe and refpect which he had for Selden and the
" reft, communicate any of the particulars to them,
" but was almoft difheartened himfelf to proceed in
" it. They were all upon their trials condemned.
" Tomkins and Challoner only were hanged. Wal-
" ler had a reprieve from General Effex; and after

" a year's imprifonment paid a fine of 10,000 *l.*
" and was pardoned."

That the reader may be enabled to judge of this
matter with the greater precifion, to this account by
Whitelocke we fhall fubjoin that of Lord Clarendon,
Hiftory, printed at Oxford, 1727, vol. II. part I. p. 247.

" There was of the Houfe of Commons," fays the
noble hiftorian, " one Mr. Waller, a gentleman of a
" very good fortune and eftate, and of admirable parts
" and faculties of wit and eloquence, and of an in-
" timate converfation and familiarity with thofe who
" had that reputation. He had, from the beginning
" of the parliament, been looked upon by all men as
" a perfon of very entire affections to the King's fer-
" vice, and to the eftablifhed government of church
" and ftate; and by having no manner of relation to
" the court, had the more credit and intereft to pro-
" **mote** the rights of it. When the ruptures grew fo
" great between the King and the two Houfes, that
" very many of the members withdrew from thofe
" counfels, he, among the reft, with equal diflike, ab-
" fented himfelf; but at the time the ftandard was
" fet up, having intimacy and friendfhip with fome
" perfons now of nearnefs about the King, with the
" King's approbation he returned again to London,
" where he fpoke, upon all occafions, with great
" fharpnefs and freedom, which (now there were fo
" few there that ufed it, and there was no danger of

" being over-voted) was not reftrained, and therefore
" ufed as an argument againft thofe who were gone
" upon pretence " that they were not fuffered to de-
" clare their opinion freely in the Houfe, which could
" not be believed, when all men knew what liberty
" Mr. Waller took, and fpoke every day with impu-
" nity againft the fenfe and proceedings of the Houfe."
" This won him a great reputation with all people
" who wifhed well to the King, and he was looked
" upon as the boldeft champion the crown had in
" both Houfes; fo that fuch Lords and Commons as
" really defired to prevent the ruin of the kingdom,
" willingly complied in a great familiarity with him,
" as a man refolute in their ends, and beft able to
" promote them: and it may be they believed his
" reputation at court fo good, that he would be no
" ill evidence there of other men's zeal and affection;
" and fo all men fpoke their minds freely to him,
" both of the general diftemper, and of the paffions
" and ambition of particular perfons; all men know-
" ing him to be of too good a fortune, and too wary
" a nature, to engage himfelf in defigns of danger or
" hazard.

" Mr. Waller had a brother-in-law, one Mr. Tom-
" kins, who had married his fifter, and was Clerk of
" the Queen's Council, of very good fame for ho-
" nefty and ability. This gentleman had good inte-
" reft and reputation in the City, and converfed much

" with thofe who difliked the proceedings of the par-
" liament, and wifhed to live under the fame govern-
" ment they were born, and from thofe citizens re-
" ceived information of the temper of the people
" upon accidents in the public affairs : and Mr. Wal-
" ler and he, with that confidence that ufes to be be-
" tween brethren of the fame good affections, fre-
" quently imparted their obfervations and opinions
" to each other, the one relating how many in both
" Houfes inclined to peace, and the other making the
" fame judgment upon the correfpondence he had,
" and intelligence he received, from the moft fubftan-
" tial men of London ; and both of them again com-
" municated what one received from the other to
" the company they ufed to converfe with ; Mr. Wal-
" ler imparting the wifhes and power of the well-
" affected party in the City to the lords and gen-
" tlemen whom he knew to be of the fame mind,
" and Mr. Tomkins acquainting thofe he durft truft
" of the City, that fuch and fuch lords and gentle-
" men, who were of fpecial note, were weary of the
" diftractions, and would heartily and confidently
" contribute to fuch an honourable and honeft peace
" as all men knew would be moft acceptable to the
" King : and from hence they came reafonably to a
" conclufion, that if fome means were found out to
" raife a confidence in thofe who wifhed well, that
" they fhould not be oppreffed by the extravagant
" power of the **defperate party, but that if they**

" would so far assist one another as to declare their
" opinions to be the same, they should be able to
" prevent or suppress those tumults which seemed
" to countenance the distractions, and the Houses
" would be induced to terms of moderation.

" In this time the Lord Conway, being returned
" from Ireland, incensed against the Scots, and dis-
" contented with the parliament here, finding Mr.
" Waller in good esteem with the Earl of Northum-
" berland, and of great friendship with the Earl of
" Portland, he entered into the same familiarity;
" and, being more of a soldier, in the discourses ad-
" ministered questions and considerations necessary
" to be understood by men that either meant to use
" force, or to resist it, and wished " that they who
" had interest and acquaintance in the City would
" endeavour, by mutual correspondence, to inform
" themselves of the distinct affections of their neigh-
" bours, that, upon any exigent, men might foresee
" whom they might trust;" and these discourses be-
" ing again derived by Mr. Waller to Mr. Tomkins,
" he, upon occasion and conference with his com-
" panions, insisted on the same arguments; and they
" again conversing with their friends and acquaint-
" ance, (for of all this business there were not above
" three who ever spoke together) agreed " that some
" well-affected persons, in every parish and ward
" about London, should make a list of all the inhabi-

B iij

" tants, and thereupon to make a reasonable guess of
" their several affections, (which at that time was no
" hard thing for observing men to do) and thence a
" computation of the strength and power of that
" party which was notoriously violent against any
" accommodation.

" I am persuaded the utmost project in this design .
" was (I speak not what particular men might intend
" or wish upon their own fancies) to beget such a com-
" bination among the party well-affected, that they
" would refuse to conform to those ordinances of
" the twentieth part, and other taxes for the support
" of the war, and thereby, or by joint petitioning for
" peace, and discountenancing the other who peti-
" tioned against it, to prevail with the parliament to
" incline to a determination of the war. And it may be
" some men might think of making advantage of any
" casual commotion, or preventing any mischief by
" it; and thereupon that inquiry where the magazines
" lay, and discourse of wearing some distinguishing
" tokens, had been rather casually mentioned than
" seriously proposed : for it is certain very many, who
" were conscious to themselves of loyal purposes to
" the King, and of hearty dislike of the parliament's
" proceedings, and observed the violent, revengeful,
" ruinating prosecution of all men by those of the
" engaged party, were not without sad apprehen-
" sions that, upon some jealousy and quarrel picked,
" even a general massacre might be attempted of all

" the King's friends; and thereupon, in several dif-
" courfes, might touch upon fuch expedients as might,
" in thofe feafons, be moft beneficial to their fafety.
" But that there was ever any formed defign, either
" of letting in the King's army into London, which
" was impoffible to be contrived, or of raifing an ar-
" my there, and furprifing the parliament, or any
" one perfon of it, or of ufing any violence in or upon
" the City, I could never yet fee caufe to **believe**;
" and if there had, they would have publifhed fuch a
" relation of it, after Mr. Waller had confeffed to them
" all he knew, had heard, or fancied to himfelf, as
" might have conftituted fome reafonable underftand-
" ing of it, and not have contented themfelves with
" making conclufions from queftions that had been
" afked, and anfwers made by perfons unknown, and
" forcing expreffions ufed by one to relate to actions of
" another, between whom there had been never the
" leaft acquaintance or correfpondence, and joining
" what was faid at London to fomewhat done at Ox-
" ford at another time, and to another purpofe; for,
" before I finifh this difcourfe, it will be neceffary to
" fpeak of another action which, how diftinct foever
" from this that is related, was woven together to
" make one plot.

" From the King's coming to Oxford, many citi-
" zens of good quality, who were profecuted, or jea-
" loufly looked upon in London, had reforted to the
" King, and hoping, if the winter produced not a

" peace, that the summer would carry the King be-
" fore that city with an army, they had entertained
" some discourse " of raising, upon their own stocks
" of money and credit, some regiments of foot and
" horse, and joining with some gentlemen of Kent,
" who were likewise inclined to such an underta-
" king." Among these was Sir Nicholas Crisp, a citizen
" of good wealth, great trade, and an active-spirited
" man, who had been lately prosecuted with great
" severity by the House of Commons, and had there-
" upon fled from London, for appearing too great a
" stickler in a petition for peace in the City. This
" gentleman industriously preserved a correspondence
" still there, by which he gave the King often very
" useful intelligence, and assured him " of a very
" considerable party which would appear there for
" him, whenever his own power should be so near as
" to give them any countenance." In the end, whe-
" ther invited by his correspondents there, or trust-
" ing his own sprightly inclinations and resolutions
" too much, and concluding that all who were equal-
" ly honest would be equally bold, he desired his Ma-
" jesty " to grant a commission to such persons, whom
" he would nominate, of the City of London, under
" the great seal of England, in the nature of a Com-
" mission of Array, by virtue whereof, when the sea-
" son should come, his party there would appear in
" discipline and order; and that this was desired by
" those who best knew what countenance and autho-

" rity was requisite, and, being trusted to them, would
" not be executed at all, or else at such a time as his
" Majesty should receive ample fruit by it, provided
" it were done with secrefy equal to the hazard they
" should run who were employed in it.

" The King had this exception to it, " the impro-
" bability that it could do good, and that the failing
" might do hurt to the undertakers." But the promo-
" ter was a very popular man in the City, where he
" had been a commander of the Trained Bands till
" the ordinance of the militia removed him, which
" rather improved than leſſened his credit, and he
" was very confident it would produce a notable ad-
" vantage to the King. However, they deſired it who
" were there, and would not appear without it ; and
" therefore the King conſented to it, referring the
" nomination of all perſons in the commiſſion to
" him, who, he verily believed, had proceeded by the
" inſtruction and advice of thoſe that were neareſt
" the concernment : and for the ſecreſy of it, the King
" referred the preparing and diſpatch of the com-
" miſſion to Sir Nicholas Criſp himſelf, who ſhould
" acquaint no more with it than he found requiſite.
" So, without the privity or advice of any counſellor
" or miniſter of ſtate then moſt truſted by his Ma-
" jeſty, he procured ſuch a commiſſion as he deſired
" (being no other than the Commiſſion of Array in
" Engliſh) to be ſigned by the King, and ſealed with
" the great ſeal.

" This being done, and remaining still in his cuf-
" tody, the Lady Aubigney, by a pafs, and with the
" confent of the Houfes, came to Oxford to transact
" the affairs of her own fortune with the King, upon
" the death of her hufband, who was killed at Edge-
" hill; and fhe having in few days difpatched her bu-
" finefs there, and being ready to return, Sir Nicho-
" las Crifp came to the King, and befought him " to
" defire that lady (who had a pafs, and fo could pro-
" mife herfelf fafety in her journey) to carry a fmall
" box (in which that commiffion fhould be) with her,
" and to keep it in her own cuftody until a gentleman
" fhould call to her Ladyfhip for it by fuch a token;
" that token, he faid, he could fend to one of the per-
" fons trufted, who fhould keep it by him till the op-
" portunity came in which it might be executed."
" The King accordingly wifhed the Lady Aubigney to
" carry it with great care and fecrefy, telling her " it
" much concerned his own fervice, and to deliver it
" in fuch manner, and upon fuch affurance, as is
" before mentioned;" which fhe did, and, within few
" days after her return to London, delivered it to a
" perfon who was appointed to call for it. How this
" commiffion was difcovered I could never learn; for
" though Mr. Waller had the honour to be admitted
" often to that lady, and was believed by her to be
" a gentleman of moft entire affections to the King's
" fervice, and, confequently, might be fitly trufted

" with what fhe knew, yet her Ladyfhip herfelf not
" knowing what it was fhe carried, could not in-
" form any body elfe.

" But about this time a fervant of Mr. Tomkins,
" who had often curforily overheard his mafter and
" Mr. Waller difcourfe of the argument we are now
" upon, placed himfelf behind a hanging at a time they
" were together, and there, whilft either of them dif-
" courfed the language and opinion of the company
" they kept, overheard enough to make him believe
" his information and difcovery would make him wel-
" come to thofe whom he thought concerned, and fo
" went to Mr. Pym, and acquainted him with all he
" had heard, or probably imagined. The time when
" Mr. Pym was made acquainted with it is not known,
" but the circumftances of the publifhing it were fuch
" as filled all men with apprehenfions. It was on
" Wednefday the 31ft of May, their folemn faft-day,
" when, being all at their fermon, in St. Margaret's
" church in Weftminfter, according to their cuftom,
" a letter or meffage is brought privately to Mr. Pym,
" who thereupon, with fome of the moft active mem-
" bers, rife from their feats, and, after a little whif-
" pering together, remove out of the church. This
" could not but exceedingly affect thofe who ftaid
" behind. Immediately they fend guards to all the
" prifons, as Lambeth-houfe, Ely-houfe, and fuch
" places, where their malignants were in cuftody, with

" directions " to search the prisoners, and some other
" places which they thought fit should be suspected."
" After the sermons were ended the Houses met, and
" were only then told, " that letters were intercepted
" going to the King and the court at Oxford, that
" expressed some notable conspiracy in hand, to de-
" liver up the parliament and the City into the hands
" of the Cavaliers, and that the time for the execu-
" tion of it drew very near." Hereupon a committee
" was appointed, " to examine all persons they
" thought fit, and to apprehend some nominated at
" that time." And the same night this committee ap-
" prehended Mr. Waller and Mr. Tomkins, and the
" next day such others as they suspected.

" Mr. Waller was so confounded with fear and ap-
" prehension, that he confessed whatever he had said,
" heard, thought, or seen; all that he knew of him-
" self, and all that he suspected of others, without
" concealing any person, of what degree or quality
" soever, or any discourse that he had ever, upon
" any occasion, entertained with them : what such
" and such ladies, of great honour, to whom, upon
" the credit of his great wit and very good reputa-
" tion he had been admitted, had spoke to him in
" their chambers of the proceedings in the Houses,
" and how they had encouraged him to oppose them;
" what correspondence and intercourse they had with
" some ministers of state at Oxford, and how they

" derived all intelligence thither. He informed them,
" " that the Earl of Portland and the Lord Conway
" had been particular in all the agitations which had
" been with the citizens, and had given frequent ad-
" vice and directions how they should demean them-
" selves; and that the Earl of Northumberland had
" expressed very good wishes to any attempt that
" might give a stop to the violent actions and proceed-
" ings of the Houses, and produce a good understand-
" ing with the King."—

" They proceeded to try Mr. Tomkins, Mr. Chal-
" loner, a citizen of good wealth and credit, and most
" intimate with Mr. Tomkins, Mr. Hambden, who
" brought the last message from the King, one Haf-
" fel, a messenger of the King's, who passed often be-
" tween London and Oxford, and sometimes carried
" letters and messages to the Lord Falkland, and
" some citizens whose names were in the commission
" sent from Oxford, by a council of war; by whom
" Mr. Tomkins and Mr. Challoner were condemned
" to be hanged, and were both, with all the circum-
" stances of severity and cruelty, executed; the one
" on a gibbet by his own house in Holborn, where he
" had long lived with singular estimation, and the
" other by his house in Cornhill, near the Old Ex-
" change. Haffel, the messenger, saved them further
" trouble, and died in prison the night before his
" trial: and there being no evidence against Mr.

" Hambden but what Mr. Waller himself gave, they
" gave no judgment against him, but kept him long
" after in prison till he died. Neither proceeded they
" capitally against those citizens whose names were
" in the commiffion, it not appearing that their names
" were ufed with their confent and privity, though
" the brand of being Malignants ferved the turn for
" their undoing; for all their eftates were feized, as
" theirs were who had been executed.

" There is nothing clearer than that the commif-
" fion fent from Oxford by the Lady Aubigney had
" not any relation to the difcourfes paffed between
" Mr. Waller, Tomkins, and thofe citizens, or that
" they who knew of one had not any privity with the
" other, which if they had had, and intended fuch
" an infurrection as was alledged, Mr. Waller, of
" Mr. Tomkins, or fome one of thofe lords who were
" fuppofed to combine with them, would have been
" in the commiffion : or if the King's minifters had
" been engaged in the confultation, and hoped to
" have raifed a party which fhould fuddenly feize
" upon the City and the parliament, they would ne-
" ver have thought a commiffion granted to fome
" gentlemen at Oxford, (for the major part of the
" Commiffioners were there) and a few private citi-
" zens, would have ferved for that work. I am very
" confident, and I have very much reafon for that con-
" fidence, that there was no more known or thought

" of at Oxford, concerning the matter of the com-
" miffion, than I have before fet forth; nor of the
" other, than that Mr. Tomkins fometimes writ to
" the Lord Falkland, (for Mr. Waller, out of the
" cautioufnefs of his own nature never writ word)
" and by meffengers fignified to him, " that the
" number of thofe who defired peace, and abhorred
" the proceedings of the Houfes, was very confider-
" able; and that they refolved, by refufing to contri-
" bute to the war, and to fubmit to their ordinances,
" to declare and manifeft themfelves in that manner,
" that the violent party in the City fhould not have
" credit enough to hinder any accommodation."
" And the Lord Falkland always returned anfwer,
" " That they fhould expedite thofe expedients as
" foon as might be, for that delays made the war
" more difficult to be reftrained." And if I could
" find evidence or reafon to induce me to believe that
" there was any further defign in the thing itfelf, or
" that the King gave further countenance to it, I
" fhould not at all conceal it. No man can imagine,
" that if the King could have entertained any pro-
" bable hope of reducing London, which was the fo-
" menter, fupporter, and indeed the life of the war,
" or could have found any expedient from whence he
" could reafonably propofe to diffolve, fcatter, and
" difperfe thofe who, under the name of a Parliament,
" had kindled a war againft him, but he would have

" given his utmost affiftance and countenance there-
" unto, either by public force or private contrivance.

" There were very great endeavours ufed to have
" proceeded with equal feverity againft the Earl of
" Portland and the Lord Conway, (for the accufa-
" tion of the Earl of Northumberland it was pro-
" ceeded tenderly in; for though the violent party
" was heartily incenfed againft him, as a man weary
" of them, yet his reputation was ftill very great)
" who were both clofe prifoners; and, to that purpofe,
" their Lordfhips and Mr. Waller were confronted
" before the committee, where they as peremptorily
" denying as he charging them, and there being no
" other witnefs but he againft them, the profecution
" was rather let alone than declined, till, after a long
" reftraint, they procured enlargement upon bail.
" Mr. Waller himfelf, (though confeffedly the moft
" guilty, and by his unhappy demeanour in this time
" of his affliction he had raifed as many enemies as
" he had formerly friends, and almoft the fame) af-
" ter he had, with incredible diffimulation, acted fuch
" a remorfe of confcience, that his trial was put off,
" out of Chriftian compaffion, till he might recover
" his underftanding, (and that was not till the heat
" and fury of the profecutors was reafonably abated
" with the facrifices they had made) and by drawing
" vifitants to himfelf of the moft powerful minifters
" of all factions, had, by his liberality and penitence,

" his receiving vulgar and vile sayings from them with
" humility and reverence, as clearer convictions and
" informations than in his life he had ever had, and
" distributing great sums to them for their prayers
" and ghostly counsel, so satisfied them that they sa-
" tisfied others, was brought, at his suit, to the House
" of Commons' bar, where, (being a man in truth
" very powerful in language, and who, by what he
" spoke, and in the manner of speaking it, exceed-
" ingly captivated the good-will and benevolence of
" his hearers, which is the highest part of an orator)
" with such flattery as was most exactly calculated to
" that meridian, with such a submission as their pride
" took delight in, and such dejection of mind and
" spirit as was like to cozen the major part, and be
" thought serious ; he laid before them " their own
" danger and concernment, if they should suffer one of
" their own body, how unworthy and monstrous so-
" ever, to be tried by the soldiers, who might thereby
" grow to that power hereafter, that they would both
" try those they would not be willing should be tried,
" and for things which they would account no crimes,
" the inconvenience and insupportable mischief where-
" of all wise commonwealths had foreseen and pre-
" vented, by exempting their own members from all
" judgments but their own." He prevailed not to be
" tried by a council of war, and thereby preserved
" his dear-bought life; so that, in truth, he does as

" much owe the keeping his head to that oration,
" as Catiline did the lofs of his to thofe of Tully * :
" and by having done ill very well, he, by degrees,
" drew that refpect to his parts which always carries
" fome compaffion to the perfon, that he got leave
" to compound for his tranfgreffion, and them to ac-
" cept of ten thoufand pounds (which their affairs
" wanted) for his liberty; whereupon he had leave
" to recollect himfelf in another country, (for his li-
" berty was to be in banifhment) how miferable he
" had made himfelf in obtaining that leave to live
" out of his own : and there cannot be a greater evi-
" dence of the ineftimable value of his parts, than
" that he lived after this in the good affection and
" efteem of many, the pity of moft, and the re-
" proach and fcorn of few or none."

After he had faved himfelf from the confequences
of this plot he travelled into France; where he continued feveral years. He went firft to Rouen in Normandy, where he refided the greater part of the time
of his banifhment. The latter years of his exile he
paffed at Paris, where he lived in gaity, in elegance,
and in the fociety of people of rank, and of thofe who
were diftinguifhed for their learning and wit.

In a fhort time after he was banifhed, an Englifh

* One would think the noble hiftorian fhould have faid,
" As Tully did the lofs of his to thofe againft Antony;"
for Catiline was flain in battle, whereas Tully's Philippics
really coft him his head.

lady of his acquaintance defired him to collect his fcattered poems, and fend them to her from France, and having complied with this lady's requifition, they were accordingly publifhed in the year 1645.

After his return from banifhment he lived chiefly at Hall-Barn, near Beaconsfield, where Cromwell ufed frequently to vifit him. Waller ufed to obferve, that when Cromwell had been called to the door in the midft of their difcourfes upon thefe fubjects, he could overhear him repeating, "The Lord will reveal, the "Lord will help," and fuch kind of cant; for which he would apologize when he came back, faying, "Cou- "fin Waller, I muft talk to thefe men after their own "way;" and would then go on where they left off. According to Waller's report, Cromwell was well verfed in the Greek and Roman hiftorians, and made obfervations upon them with uncommon penetration and tafte: and though we do not find that Cromwell trufted any part of the public bufinefs to Waller's management, yet he treated him with refpect and kindnefs.

At the reftoration he was treated with great civility by Charles II. who always made him one of the party in his diverfions at the Duke of Buckingham's and other places, and gave him a grant of the Pro- voftfhip of Eton College, though that grant proved of no effect, Lord Clarendon, who was then Lord Chancel- lor, refufing to affix the feal to the patent, alledging that a layman could not legally hold the Provoſtſhip. The King having one day obſerved to Waller, that he thought his poem on his return inferior to his pancygric upon Cromwell, Waller made this memorable reply; "Sir," ſays he, " poets always ſucceed " better in compoſing fiction than in adorning truth."

He ſat in ſeveral parliaments after the reſtoration, and continued in the full vigour of genius to the end of his life, and his natural vivacity made his company agreeable to the laſt. James II. notwithſtanding the bigotry and gloomineſs of his mind, affected to be an admirer of Waller, and having one day ordered the Earl of Sunderland to bring Waller to him in the afternoon, when he came the King carried him into his cloſet, and there aſked him how he liked ſuch a picture? " Sir," ſays Mr. Waller, " my eyes are dim, " and I know not whoſe it is." " It is the Princeſs " of Orange," replied the King. " And ſhe is like " the greateſt woman in the world," ſays the poet. " Whom do you call ſo?" aſked the King. " Queen " Elizabeth," anſwered Waller. " I wonder," rejoined the King, " you ſhould think ſo; but I muſt " confeſs ſhe had a wiſe council." " And, Sir," demanded Waller in his turn, " did your Majeſty " ever know a fool chuſe a wiſe one?"

In ſummer 1687 he was attacked with a ſwelling in his legs. In autumn of ſame year the diſorder increaſing confined him to bed, and he found his life drawing to a period : for this awful event he prepared himself, and supported the last scene of life with propriety and fortitude. He died on the 21st of October 1687, and was interred in the churchyard of Beaconsfield.

He left several children, and bequeathed his estate to his second son Edmund, his eldest, Benjamin, being so far from inheriting his father's wit, that he even wanted common sense. He was sent to New-Jersey in America. Edmund, in the beginning of his life, was member of parliament for Agmondesham, but afterwards turned Quaker. He died without issue, and left the estate to Edmund, the eldest son of his brother Dr. Stephen Waller, who was our Poet's fourth son, and a famous Civilian. By his first wife our Author had a son and a daughter; and by his second wife, Mary, of the family of Bresse, or Breaux, in the province of Normandy, he had five sons and eight daughters, most of whom survived him.

Waller's person was elegant and graceful; and his elocution, like his verse, was musical and flowing. So happily formed was he for society, that his conversation, which was at once polite, learned, and witty, was courted by those who detested his principles and conduct. But as the character of this Poet is drawn at large by the masterly hand of Lord Clarendon, the reader will find it includes every thing that needs be said in regard to him. " Edmund Waller," says

the noble hiftorian, " was born to a very fair eftate,
" by the parfimony or frugality of a wife father
" and mother, and he thought it fo commendable an
" advantage, that he refolved to improve it with his
" utmoft care, upon which in his nature he was too
" much intent ; and, in order to that, he was fo much
" referved and retired, that he was fcarce ever heard
" of till, by his addrefs and dexterity, he had gotten
" a very rich wife in the City, againft all the recom-
" mendation, and countenance, and authority, of the
" court, which was thorougly engaged on the be-
" half of Mr. Crofts, and which ufed to be fuccefsful,
" in that age, againft any oppofition. He had the good
" fortune to have an alliance and friendfhip with Dr.
" Morley, who had affifted and inftructed him in the
" reading many good books, to which his natural
" parts and promptitude inclined him, efpecially the
" Poets; and at the age when other men ufed to give
" over writing verfes, (for he was near thirty years
" of age when he firft engaged himfelf in that excr-
" cife, at leaft that he was known to do fo) he fur-
" prifed the Town with two or three pieces of that
" kind, as if a tenth Mufe had been newly born to
" cherifh drooping poetry. The Doctor at that time
" brought him into that company which was moft
" celebrated for good converfation, where he was
" received and efteemed with great applaufe and
" refpect. He was a very pleafant difcourfer, in ear-

" neſt, and in jeſt, and therefore very grateful to
" all kind of company, where he was not the leſs
" eſteemed for being very rich. He had been even
" nurſed in parliaments, where he ſat when he was
" very young, and ſo when they were reſumed again,
" (after a long intermiſſion) he appeared in thoſe aſ-
" ſemblies with great advantage. Having a graceful
" way of ſpeaking, and by thinking much upon ſeve-
" ral arguments (which his temper and complexion,
" that had much of melancholic, inclined him to)
" he ſeemed often to ſpeak upon the ſudden, when
" the occaſion had only adminiſtered the opportu-
" nity of ſaying what he had thoroughly conſidered,
" which gave a great luſtre to all he ſaid, which yet
" was rather of delight than weight. There needs
" no more be ſaid to extol the excellence and power
" of his wit, and pleaſantneſs of his converſation,
" than that it was of magnitude enough to cover a
" world of very great faults ; that is, ſo to cover them,
" that they were not taken notice of to his reproach;
" viz. a narrowneſs in his nature to the loweſt degree;
" an abjectneſs and want of courage to ſupport him
" in any virtuous undertaking; an inſinuation and
" ſervile flattery to the height the vaineſt and moſt
" imperious nature could be contented with ; that it
" preſerved and won his life from thoſe who were
" moſt reſolved to take it, and on an occaſion in
" which he ought to have been ambitious to have loſt

" it, and then preferved him again from the reproach
" and contempt that was due to him for fo prefer-
" ving it, and for vindicating it at fuch a price; that
" it had power to reconcile him to thofe whom he
" had moft offended and provoked, and continued
" to his old age with that rare felicity, that his com-
" pany was acceptable when his fpirit was odious, and
" he was at leaft pitied where he was moft detefted."

But however unfavourably we are obliged to think
of Mr. Waller's virtues and moral accomplifhments,
yet that he greatly improved our language and verfi-
fication, and that his Works gave a new era to Englifh
poetry, was allowed by his cotemporaries, nor has it
ever been difputed by good critics. The anonymous
author of the Preface to the Second part of his poems,
printed in the 1690, has fpoken pertinently to this
part of his character: " Mr. Waller's is a name," fays
he, " that carries every thing in it that is either great or
" graceful in poetry. He was, indeed, the parent of
" Englifh verfe, and the firft that fhewed us our tongue
" had beauty and numbers in it. Our language owes
" more to him than the French does to Cardinal
" Richelieu and the whole Academy.——The tongue
" came into his hands like a rough diamond : he po-
" lifhed it firft, and to that degree, that all artifts
" fince him have admired the workmanfhip, without
" pretending to mend it. Suckling and Carew, I
" muft confefs, wrote fome few things fmoothly

5

" enough; but as all they did in this kind was not
" very confiderable, fo it was a little later than the
" earlieſt pieces of Mr. Waller. He undoubtedly ſtands
" firſt in the liſt of refiners, and, for ought I know, laſt
" too; for I queſtion whether in Charles II.'s reign
" Engliſh did not come to its full perfection, and
" whether it has not had its Auguſtan age as well as
" the Latin. It feems to be already mixed with the
" foreign languages as far as its purity will bear; and,
" as chymiſts fay of their menſtruums, to be quite
" fated with the infuſion. But poſterity will beſt
" judge of this. In the mean time, it is a furpriſing
" reflection, that between what Spenſer wrote laſt,
" and Waller firſt, there ſhould not be much above
" twenty years' diſtance; and yet the one's language,
" like the money of that time, is as current now as
" ever; whilſt the other's words are like old coins,
" one muſt go to an antiquary to underſtand their
" true meaning and value. Such advances may a
" great genius make when it undertakes any thing
" in earneſt !"

Waller's Works will always hold a confiderable rank
in Engliſh poetry, and his great abilities as an orator are indiſputable; and though, as Mr. Stockdale
obſerves, " his behaviour on his trial was hypocri-
" tical, unmanly, and abject; yet the alarming oc-
" caſion of it, on which but few would have acquitted
" themſelves with a determined fortitude, extenu-

" ates it in some measure to candour and humanity.
" ——Let us not condemn him with untempered se-
" verity, because he was not a prodigy which the
" world hath seldom seen; because his character com-
" prised not the poet, the orator, and the hero.——
" His moral character will be viewed with lenity by
" those whose minds are actuated by humanity, and
" who are properly acquainted with their own fail-
" ings; who consider the violence of the times in
" which he lived, and who are accustomed to think
" before they decide."

---

*The epitaph on Mr. Waller's monument in Beaconsfield
churchyard in Buckinghamshire, written by Mr. Rymer,
late Historiographer-royal.*

ON THE WEST END.

Edmundi Waller hic jacet id quantum
Morti cessit; qui inter poetas sui
Temporis facilè princeps, lauream, quam
Meruit adolescens, octogenarius haud
Abdicavit. Huic debet patria lingua
Quod credas, si Græcè Latinèque
Intermitterent, Musæ loqui amarent
Anglicè.

ON THE SOUTH SIDE.

Heus, Viator! tumulatum vides
Edmundum Waller qui tanti nominis
Poeta, et idem avitis opibus, inter primos
Spectabilis, Musis se dedit, et patriæ.
Nondum octodecenalis, inter ardua
    Regni tractantes sedem habuit, à
Burgo de Agmondesham missus. **Hic vitæ**
Cursus; nec oneri defuit senex; vixitque
Semper populo charus, principibus in
    Deliciis, admirationi omnibus.
Hic conditur tumulo sub eodem rara
Virtute et multa prole nobilis uxor,
    Maria ex Bressyorum familia, cum
Edmundo Waller, conjuge charissimo:
Quem ter et decies lætum fecit patrem,
V filiis, filiabus viii; quos mundo dedit,
    Et in cœlum rediit.

ON THE EAST END.

Edmundus Waller cui hoc marmor
Sacrum est, Coleshill nascendi locum
Habuit; Cantabrigiam studendi; patrem
Robertum et ex Hampdena stirpe matrem:
    Cœpit vivere iii° Martii, A. D. 1605.
Prima uxor Anna Edwardi Banks filia
Unica hæres. **Ex** prima bis pater factus;
Ex secunda tredecies; cui et duo lustra
Superstes, obiit **xxi** Octob. A. D. 1687,

ON THE NORTH SIDE.

Hoc marmore Edmundo Waller
Mariæque ex secundis nuptiis conjugi,
Pientissimis parentibus, piissimè
Parentavit Edmundus filius. Honores
Bene-merentibus extremos dedit quos
Ipse fugit. El. W. I. F. H. G. Ex testamento
H. M. P. in Jul. 1700.

WHEN the Author of these verses (written only to please himself, and such particular persons to whom they were directed) returned from abroad some years since, he was troubled to find his name in print, but somewhat satisfied to see his lines so ill rendered that he might justly disown them, and say to a mistaking printer as * one did to an ill reciter,

*** Male dum recitas, incipit esse tuus.

Having been ever since pressed to correct the many and gross faults, (such as use to be in impressions wholly neglected by the authors) his answer was, that he made these when ill verses had more favour, and escaped better, than good ones do in this age; the severity whereof he thought not unhappily diverted by those faults in the impression which hitherto have hung upon his book, as the Turks hang old rags, or such like ugly things, upon their fairest horses, and other goodly creatures, to secure them against fascination. And for those of a more confined understanding, who pretend not to censure, as they admire most what they least comprehend, so his verses (maimed to that degree that himself scarce knew what to make of many of them) might, that way at least, have a title to some admiration; which is no small matter, if what an old author

* Martial, lib. i. ep. 39.

D iij

obferves be true, that the aim of orators is victory, of hiftorians truth, and of poets admiration. He had reafon, therefore, to indulge thofe faults in his book, whereby it might be reconciled to fome, and commended to others.

The printer alfo, he thought, would fare the worfe if thofe faults were amended; for we fee maimed ftatues fell better than whole ones; and clipped and wafhed money goes about, when the entire and weighty lies hoarded up.

Thefe are the reafons which, for above twelve years paft, he has oppofed to our requeft; to which it was replied, that as it would be too late to recall that which had fo long been made public, fo might it find excufe from his youth, the feafon it was produced in: and for what had been done fince, and now added, if it commend not his poetry, it might his philofophy, which teaches him fo cheerfully to bear fo great a calamity as the lofs of the beft part of his fortune, torn from him in prifon, (in which, and in banifhment, the beft portion of his life hath alfo been fpent) that he can ftill fing under the burthen, not unlike that Roman *,

* * * Quem demifere Philippi
Decifis humilem pennis, inopemque paterni
Et laris et fundi. * * *

Whofe fpreading wings the Civil war had clipp'd,
And him of his old patrimony ftripp'd.

* Horace, lib. ii. ep. 2.

Who yet not long after could fay,

> Mufis amicus, triftitiam et metus
> Tradam protervis in mare Creticum
> Portare ventis. * * * Lib. i. ode 26.
>
> They that acquainted with the Mufes be,
> Send care and forrow by the winds to fea.

Not fo much moved with thefe reafons of ours, (or pleafed with our rhymes) as wearied with our importunity, he has at laft given us leave to affure the reader that the Poems which have been fo long and fo ill fet forth under his name, are here to be found as he firft writ them; as alfo to add fome others which have fince been compofed by him: and though his advice to the contrary might have difcouraged us, yet obferving how often they have been reprinted, what price they have borne, and how earneftly they have been always inquired after, but efpecially of late, (making good that of Horace,

> * * * Meliora dies, ut vina, poemata reddit. Lib. ii. ep. 1.

" fome verfes being, like fome wines, recommended " to our tafte by time and age") we have adventured upon this new and well-corrected edition, which, for our own fakes as well as thine, we hope will fucceed better than he apprehended.

> Vivitur ingenio, caetera mortis erunt.
>
> ALBINOVANUS.

THE reader needs be told no more in commendation of these Poems, than that they are Mr. Waller's, a name that carries every thing in it that is either great or graceful in poetry. He was, indeed, the parent of English verse, and the first that shewed us our tongue had beauty and numbers in it. Our language owes more to him than the French does to Cardinal Richelieu and the whole Academy. A poet cannot think of him without being in the same rapture Lucretius is in when Epicurus comes in his way.

> Tu pater, et rerum inventor; tu patria nobis
> Suppeditas praecepta: tuisque ex, Inclute! chartis,
> Floriferis ut apes in saltibus omnia libant,
> Omnia nos itidem depascimur aurea dicta;
> Aurea! perpetua semper dignissima vita!   Lib. iii. ver. 9.

The tongue came into his hands like a rough diamond: he polished it first, and to that degree, that all artists since him have admired the workmanship, without pretending to mend it. Suckling and Carew, I must confess, wrote some few things smoothly enough; but as all they did in this kind was not very considerable, so it was a little later than the earliest pieces of Mr. Waller. He undoubtedly stands first in the list of refiners, and, for ought I know, last too; for I question whether in Charles II.'s reign English did not come to its full perfection, and whether it has

not had its Auguftan age as well as the Latin. It
feems to be already mixed with foreign languages as
far as its purity will bear; and, as chymifts fay of
their menftruums, to be quite fated with the infufion.
But pofterity will beft judge of this. In the mean
time, it is a furprifing reflection, that between what
Spenfer wrote laft, and Waller firft, there fhould not
be much above twenty years' diftance; and yet the
one's language, like the money of that time, is as current now as ever; whilft the other's words are like
old coins, one muft go to an antiquary to underftand
their true meaning and value. Such advances may a
great genius make when it undertakes any thing in
earneft!

Some painters will hit the chief lines and mafter-
ftrokes of a face fo truly, that thro' all the differences
of age the picture fhall ftill bear a refemblance. This
art was Mr. Waller's: he fought out, in this flowing
tongue of ours, what parts would laft, and be of
ftanding ufe and ornament; and this he did fo fuc-
cefsfully, that his language is now as frefh as it was
at firft fetting out. Were we to judge barely by the
wording, we could not know what was wrote at twenty, and what at fourfcore. He complains, indeed, of
a tide of words that comes in upon the Englifh poet,
and overflows whatever he builds; but this was lefs
his cafe than any man's that ever wrote; and the
mifchief of it is, this very complaint will laft long

enough to confute itfelf; for though Englifh be moul-
dering ftone, as he tells us there, yet he has certainly
picked the beft out of a bad quarry.

We are no lefs beholden to him for the new turn
of verfe which he brought in, and the improvement
he made in our numbers. Before his time men rhymed indeed, and that was all : as for the harmony of
meafure, and that dance of words which good ears
are fo much pleafed with, they knew nothing of it.
Their poetry then was made up almoft entirely of
monofyllables, which, when they come together in
any clufter, are certainly the moft harfh, untuneable
things in the world. If any man doubts of this, let
him read ten lines in Donne, and he will be quickly
convinced. Befides, their verfes ran all into one another, and hung together, throughout a whole copy,
like the hooked atoms that compofe a body in Des
Cartes. There was no diftinction of parts, no regular
ftops, nothing for the ear to reft upon; but as foon
as the copy began, down it went like a larum, incef-
fantly, and the reader was fure to be out of breath
before he got to the end of it : fo that really verfe,
in thofe days, was but down-right profe tagged with
rhymes. Mr. Waller removed all thefe faults, brought
in more polyfyllables, and fmoother meafures, bound
up his thoughts better, and in a cadence more agreeable to the nature of the verfe he wrote in; fo that
wherever the natural ftops of that were, he contri-

ted the little breakings of his fenfe fo as to fall in
with them; and, for that reafon, fince the ftrefs of
our verfe lies commonly upon the laft fyllable, you
will hardly ever find him ufing a word of no force
there. I would fay, if I were not afraid the reader
would think me too nice, that he commonly clofes
with verbs, in which we know the life of language
confifts.

Among other improvements we may reckon that
of his rhymes, which are always good, and very often
the better for being new. He had a fine ear, and
knew how quickly that fenfe was cloyed by the fame
round of chiming words ftill returning upon it. It is
a decided cafe by the great mafter of writing *, *Quæ
funt ampla, et pulchra, diu placere poffunt ; quæ lepida
et concinna*, (amongft which rhyme muft, whether it
will or no, take its place) *citò fatietate afficiunt au-
rium fenfum faftidiofiffimum*. This he underftood very
well; and therefore, to take off the danger of a furfeit that way, ftrove to pleafe by variety and new
founds. Had he carried this obfervation, among others,
as far as it would go, it muft, methinks, have fhown
him the incurable fault of this jingling kind of poetry,
and have led his later judgment to blank verfe: but
he continued an obftinate lover of rhyme to the very
laft: it was a miftrefs that never appeared unhand-
fome in his eyes, and was courted by him long after

* Ad Herennium, lib. iv.

Sacharissa was forsaken. He had raised it, and brought it to that perfection we now enjoy it in ; and the poet's temper (which has always a little vanity in it) would not suffer him ever to slight a thing he had taken so much pains to adorn. My Lord Roscommon was more impartial ; no man ever rhymed truer and evener than he ; yet he is so just as to confess that it is but a trifle, and to wish the tyrant dethroned, and blank verse set up in its room. There is a third person *, the living glory of our English poetry, who has disclaimed the use of it upon the stage, tho' no man ever employed it there so happily as he. It was the strength of his genius that first brought it into credit in Plays, and it is the force of his example that has thrown it out again. In other kinds of writing it continues still, and will do so till some excellent spirit arises that has leisure enough, and resolution, to break the charm, and free us from the troublesome bondage of rhyming, as Mr. Milton very well calls it, and has proved it as well by what he has wrote in another way. But this is a thought for times at some distance ; the present age is a little too warlike ; it may perhaps furnish out matter for a good poem in the next, but it will hardly encourage one now. Without prophesying, a man may easily know what sort of laurels are like to be in request.

* Mr. Dryden.

Whilst I am talking of verse, I find myself, I do not know how, betrayed into a great deal of prose. I intended no more than to put the reader in mind what respect was due to any thing that fell from the pen of Mr. Waller. I have heard his last-printed copies, which are added in the several editions of his poems. very slightly spoken of, but certainly they do not deserve it : they do indeed discover themselves to be his last, and that is the worst we can say of them. He is there

Jam senior; sed cruda Deo viridisque senectus*.

The same censure, perhaps, will be passed on the pieces of this Second Part. I shall not so far engage for them, as to pretend they are all equal to whatever he wrote in the vigour of his youth ; yet they are so much of a piece with the rest, that any man will at first sight know them to be Mr. Waller's. Some of them were wrote very early, but not put into former collections, for reasons obvious enough, but which are now ceased. The play was altered to please the court: it is not to be doubted who sat for the Two Brothers' characters. It was agreeable to the sweetness of Mr. Waller's temper to soften the rigour of the tragedy, as he expresses it ; but whether it be so agreeable to the nature of tragedy itself to make every thing come off easily, I leave to the critics. In the prologue and

* Virg. Aen. vi. v. 304.

epilogue there are a few verses that he has made use
of upon another occasion; but the reader may be
pleased to allow that in him that has been allowed
so long in Homer and Lucretius. Exact writers dress
up their thoughts so very well always, that when they
have need of the same sense, they cannot put it into
other words but it must be to its prejudice. Care has
been taken, in this book, to get together every thing
of Mr. Waller's that is not put into the former collection; so that between both the reader may make
the set complete.

It will, perhaps, be contended, after all, that some
of these ought not to have been published; and Mr.
Cowley's * decision will be urged, that a neat tomb
of marble is a better monument than a great pile of
rubbish. It might be answered to this, that the pic-
tures and poems of great masters have been always
valued, though the last hand were not put to them :
and I believe none of those gentlemen that will make
the objection would refuse a sketch of Raphael's, or
one of Titian's draughts of the first sitting. I might
tell them, too, what care has been taken, by the
learned, to preserve the fragments of the ancient
Greek and Latin poets : there has been thought to
be a divinity in what they said; and therefore the
least pieces of it have been kept up and reverenced
like religious reliques : and I am sure, take away the

* In the preface to his works.

mille anni *, and impartial reafoning will tell us there is as much due to the memory of Mr. Waller, as to the moft celebrated names of Antiquity.

But, to wave the difpute now of what *ought* to have been done, I can affure the reader what *would* have been, had this edition been delayed. The following Poems were got abroad, and in a great many hands : it were vain to expect that, among fo many admirers of Mr. Waller, they fhould not meet with one fond enough to publifh them. They might have ftaid, indeed, 'till by frequent tranfcriptions they had been corrupted extremely, and jumbled together with things of another kind; but then they would have found their way into the world : fo it was thought a greater piece of kindnefs to the Author to put them out whilft they continue genuine and unmixed, and fuch as he himfelf, were he alive, might own.

---

* Alluding to that verfe in Juvenal,

     * * * Et nni cedit Homero
     Propter mille annos * * *   Sat. 7.

And yields to Homer on no other fcore,
Than that he liv'd a thoufand years before.   Mr. C. Dryden.

LADY MARGARET-CAVENDISH HARLEY.

Let others boaft the Nine Aonian maids,
Infpiring ftreams, and fweet refounding fhades,
Where Phœbus heard the rival bards rehearfe,
And bade the laurels learn the lofty verfe:
In vain! nor Phœbus nor the boafted Nine
Inflame the raptur'd foul with rays divine:
None but the fair intufe the facred fire,
And love with vocal art informs the lyre.

When Waller, kindling with celeftial rage,
View'd the bright Harley of that wond'ring age,
His pleafing pain he taught the lute to breathe;
The Graces fung, and wove his myrtle wreath.
In youth, of patrimonial wealth poffeft,
The praife of fcience faintly warm'd his breaft;
But, fir'd to fame by Sidney's rofy fmile,
Swift o'er the laureat realm he urg'd his toil.
His Mufe, by Nature form'd to pleafe the fair,
Or fing of heroes with majeflic air,
To melting ftrains attun'd her voice, and ftrove
To waken all the tender powers of love:
More fweetly foft her awful beauty fhone,
Than Juno grac'd with Cytherea's zone.

As angels love, congenial fouls unite
Their radiance, and refine each other's light:

The florid and fublime, the grave and gay,
From Waller's beams imbibe a purer ray;
Illumin'd thence in equal lays to bound
Their copious fenfe, and harmonize the found;
With varied notes the curious ear to pleafe,
And turn a nervous thought with artful eafe.
Maker and model of melodious verfe!
Accept thefe votive honours at thy herfe.
While I with filial awe attempt thy praife,
Infufe thy genius, and my fancy raife!
So, warbling o'er his urn, the woodland choirs
To Orpheus pay the fong his fhade infpires.

In Waller's fame, O faireft Harley! view
What verdant palms fhall owe their birth to you:
To you what deathlefs charms are thence decreed,
In Sachariffa's fate vouchfafe to read.
Secure beneath the wing of with'ring Time,
Her beauties flourifh in ambrofial prime:
Still kindling rapture, fee! fhe moves in ftate;
Gods, nymphs, and heroes, on her triumph wait.
Nor think the lover's praife of love's delight,
In pureft minds may ftain the virgin-white:
How bright and chafte the poet and his theme!
So Cynthia fhines on Arethufa's ftream.
A fainted virtue to the fpheres may fing
Thofe ftrains that ravifh'd here the Martyr-king.
Plenteous of native wit, in letter'd eafe
Politely form'd, to profit and to pleafe,

E iij

To Fame whate'er was due he gave to Fame,
And what he could not praise forgot to name:
Thus Eden's rose without a thorn display'd
Her bloom, and in a fragrant blush decay'd.

 Such soul-attracting airs were sung of old,
When blissful years in golden circles roll'd:
Pure from deceit, devoid of fear and strife,
While love was all the pensive care of life,
The swains in green retreats, with flowrets crown'd,
Taught the young groves their passion to resound:
Fancy pursu'd the paths where Beauty led,
To please the living, or deplore the dead:
While to their warbled woe the rocks reply'd,
The rills remurmur'd, and the zephyrs sigh'd;
From death redeem'd by verse, the vanish'd fair
Breath'd in a flow'r, or sparkled in a star.
Bright as the stars, and fragrant as the flow'rs,
Where Spring resides in soft Elysian bow'rs;
While these the bow'rs adorn, and they the sphere,
Will Sacharissa's charms in song appear.
Yet, in the present age, her radiant name
Must take a dimmer interval of fame;
When you to full meridian lustre rise,
With Morton's shape and Gloriana's eyes,
With Carlisle's wit, her gesture, and her mien,
And, like seraphic Rich, with zeal serene;
In sweet assemblage all their graces join'd
To language, mode, and manners, more refin'd!

That angel-frame, with chaſte attraction gay,
Mild as the dove-ey'd Morn awakes the May,
Of nobleſt youths will reign the public care,
Their joy, their wiſh, their wonder, and deſpair.
Far-beaming thence what bright ideas flow!
The ſiſter-arts with ſudden rapture glow:
Her Titian tints the Painter nymph reſumes;
The canvaſs warm with roſeate beauty blooms:
Inſpir'd with life by Sculpture's happy toil,
The marble breathes, and ſoftens with your ſmile;
Proud to receive the form, by Fate deſign'd
The faireſt model of the fairer kind.
But hear, O hear the Muſe's heav'nly voice!
The waving woods and echoing vales rejoice:
Attend, ye Gales! to Margaretta's praiſe,
And all ye liſt'ning Loves record the lays!
So Philomela charms th' Idalian grove,
When Venus, in the glowing orb of love,
O'er ocean, earth, and air, extends her reign,
The firſt, the brighteſt, of the ſtarry train.

What fav'rite youth aſſign the Fates to riſe,
In bridal pomp to lead the blooming prize?
Whether his father's garter'd ſhield ſuſtains
Trophies achieved on Gallia's viny plains,
Or ſmiling Peace a mingled wreath diſplays,
The patriot's olive, and the poet's bays:
Adorn, ye Fates! the fav'rite youth aſſign'd
With each ennobling grace of form and mind:

In merit make him great, as great in blood;
Great without pride, and amiably good:
His breaſt the guardian ark of heav'n-born law,
To ſtrike a faithleſs age with conſcious awe:
In choice of friends by manly reaſon ſway'd;
Not fear'd, but honour'd, and with love obey'd.
In courts and camps, in council and retreat,
Wiſe, brave, and ſtudious to ſupport the ſtate;
With candour firm; without ambition bold,
No deed diſcolour'd with the guilt of gold;
That Heav'n may judge the choiceſt bleſſings due,
And give the various good compris'd in you.

E. FENTON.

I.

OF THE DANGER

HIS MAJESTY [BEING PRINCE]

ESCAPED IN THE ROAD AT ST. ANDERO.

Now had his Highnefs bid farewell to Spain,
And reach'd the fphere of his own pow'r, the main:
With Britifh bounty in his fhip he feafts
Th' Hefperian princes, his amazed guefts,
To find that watry wildernefs exceed **5**
The entertainment of their great Madrid.
Healths to both kings, attended with the roar
Of cannons, echo'd from th' affrighted fhore,
With loud refemblance of his thunder, prove
Bacchus the feed of cloud-compelling Jove; **10**
While to his harp divine Arion fings
The loves and conquefts of our Albion kings.

 Of the Fourth Edward was his noble fong,
Fierce, goodly, valiant, beautiful, and young:
He rent the crown from vanquifh'd Henry's head,**15**
Rais'd the White Rofe, and trampled on the Red:
'Till Love, triumphing o'er the victor's pride,
Brought Mars and Warwick to the conquer'd fide:

Neglected Warwick (whose bold hand, like Fate,
Gives and resumes the sceptre of our state)　　20
Wooes for his master; and with double shame,
Himself deluded, mocks the princely dame,
The Lady Bona whom just anger burns,
And foreign war with civil rage returns.
Ah! spare your swords, where beauty is to blame; 25
Love gave th' affront, and must repair the fame:
When France shall boast of her, whose conqu'ring eyes
Have made the best of English hearts their prize;
Have pow'r to alter the decrees of Fate,
And change again the counsels of our state.　　30
　　What the prophetic Muse intends, alone
To him that feels the secret wound is known.
　　With the sweet sound of this harmonious lay,
About the keel delighted dolphins play,
Too sure a sign of sea's ensuing rage,　　　35
Which must anon this royal troop engage;
To whom soft sleep seems more secure and sweet,
Within the town commanded by our fleet.
　　These mighty peers plac'd in the gilded barge,
Proud with the burden of so brave a charge,　40
With painted oars the youths begin to sweep
Neptune's smooth face, and cleave the yielding deep;
Which soon becomes the seat of sudden war
Between the wind and tide that fiercely jar.
As when a sort of lusty shepherds try　　　45
Their force at foot-ball, care of victory

Makes them salute so rudely breast to breast,
That their encounter seems too rough for jest;
They ply their feet, and still the restless ball,
'Toss'd to and fro, is urged by them all: 50
So fares the doubtful barge 'twixt tide and **winds,**
And like effect of their contention finds.
Yet the bold Britons still securely row'd;
Charles and his virtue was their sacred load;
Than which a greater pledge Heav'n could not give, 55
That the good boat this tempest should out-live.
But storms increase, and now no hope of grace
Among them shines, save in the Prince's face;
The rest resign their courage, skill, and sight,
To danger, horror, and unwelcome night. 60
The gentle vessel, (wont with state and pride
On the smooth back of silver Thames to ride)
Wanders astonish'd in the angry main,
As Titan's car did, while the golden rein
Fill'd the young hand of his advent'rous son *, 65
When the whole world an equal hazard run
To this of ours, the light of whose desire
Waves threaten now, as that was scar'd by fire.
Th' impatient Sea grows impotent and raves,
That, Night assisting, his impetuous waves 70
Should find resistance from so light a thing;
These surges ruin, those our safety bring.
Th' oppressed vessel doth the charge abide,
Only because assail'd on every side:

* Phaeton.

So men with rage and passion set on fire,   75
Trembling for haste, impeach their mad desire.

   The pale Iberians had expir'd with fear,
But that their wonder did divert their care,
To see the Prince with danger mov'd no more
Than with the pleasures of their court before: 80
Godlike his courage seem'd, whom nor delight
Could soften, nor the face of Death affright.
Next to the pow'r of making tempests cease,
Was in that storm to have so calm a peace.
Great Maro could no greater tempest feign,   85
When the loud winds usurping on the main
For angry Juno, labour'd to destroy
The hated reliques of confounded Troy:
His bold Æneas, on like billows tost
In a tall ship, and all his country lost,   90
Dissolves with fear; and both his hands upheld,
Proclaims them happy whom the Greeks had quell'd
In honourable fight : our hero, set
In a small shallop, Fortune in his debt,
So near a hope of crowns and sceptres, more   95
Than ever Priam, when he flourished, wore;
His loins yet full of ungot princes, all
His glory in the bud, lets nothing fall
That argues fear : if any thought annoys
The gallant youth, 'tis love's untasted joys,   100
And dear remembrance of that fatal glance,
For which he lately pawn'd his heart in France;

Where he had seen a brighter nymph than she *
That sprung out of his present foe, the sea.
That noble ardour, more than mortal fire,   105
The conquer'd ocean could not make expire;
Nor angry Thetis raise her waves above
Th' heroic Prince's courage or his love :
'Twas indignation, and not fear he felt,
The shrine should perish where that image dwelt.110
Ah, Love forbid! the noblest of thy train
Should not survive to let her know his pain;
Who nor his peril minding nor his flame,
Is entertain'd with some less serious game,
Among the bright nymphs of the Gallic court, 115
All highly born, obsequious to her sport :
They roses seem, which in their early pride
But half reveal, and half their beauties hide;
She the glad morning, which her beams does throw
Upon their smiling leaves, and gilds them so ;   120
Like bright Aurora, whose refulgent ray
Fortels the fervour of ensuing day,
And warns the shepherd with his flocks retreat
To leafy shadows from the threaten'd heat.

From Cupid's string of many shafts, that fled 125
Wing'd with those plumes which noble Fame had shed,
As thro' the wond'ring world she flew, and told
Of his adventures, haughty, brave, and bold;

* Venus.

Some had already touch'd the royal maid,
But Love's first summons seldom are obey'd :　130
Light was the wound, the Prince's care unknown,
She might not, would not, yet reveal her own.
His glorious name had so possest her ears,
That with delight those antique tales she hears
Of Jason, Theseus, and such worthies old,　　135
As with his story best resemblance hold.
And now she views, as on the wall it hung,
What old Musæus so divinely sung;
Which art with life and love did so infpire,
That she discerns and favours that desire;　　140
Which there provokes th' advent'rous youth to swim,
And in Leander's danger pities him;
Whose not new love alone, but fortune, seeks
To frame his story like that amorous Greek's.
For from the stern of some good ship appears　145
A friendly light, which moderates their fears :
New courage from reviving hope they take,
And climbing o'er the waves that taper make;
On which the hope of all their lives depends,
As his on that fair Hero's hand extends.　　150
The ship at anchor, like a fixed rock,
Breaks the proud billows which her large sides knock;
Whose rage restrained, foaming higher swells,
And from her port the weary barge repels,
Threat'ning to make her, forced out again,　　155
Repeat the dangers of the troubled main.

Twice was the cable hurl'd in vain; the Fates
Would not be moved for our fifter ftates.
For England is the third fuccefsful throw,
And then the genius of that land they know,   160
Whofe prince muft be (as their own books devife)
Lord of the fcene where now his danger lies.

   Well fung the Roman bard, " All human things
" Of deareft value hang on flender ftrings."
O fee the then fole hope, and, in defign   165
Of Heav'n, **our** joy, fupported by a line !
Which **for** that inftant was Heav'n's care above,
The chain that's fixed to the throne of Jove,
On which the fabric of our world depends,
One link diffolv'd, the whole creation ends.   170

II.

OF HIS MAJESTY'S

RECEIVING THE NEWS OF THE

DUKE OF BUCKINGHAM'S DEATH.

So earneft with thy God! can no new care,
No fenfe of danger, interrupt thy pray'r ?
The facred Wreftler, till a bleffing giv'n,
Quits not his hold, but halting conquers Heav'n.
Nor was the ftream of thy devotion ftopp'd,   5
When from the body fuch a limb was lopp'd,
As to thy prefent ftate was no lefs maim,
Tho' thy wife choice has fince repair'd the fame.

Bold Homer durft not fo great virtue feign
In his beft pattern * : of Patroclus flain,   10
With fuch amazement as weak mothers ufe,
And frantic gefture, he receives the news.
Yet fell his darling by th' impartial chance
Of war, impos'd by royal Hector's lance;
Thine in full peace, and by a vulgar hand   15
Torn from thy bofom, left his high command.

    The famous painter † could allow no place
For private forrow in a prince's face:
Yet, that his piece might not exceed belief,
He caft a veil upon fuppofed grief.   20
'Twas want of fuch a precedent as this
Made the old Heathen frame their gods amifs.
Their Phœbus fhould not act a fonder part
For the fair boy ‡, than he did for his hart;   24
Nor blame for Hyacinthus' fate his own,   [known.
That kept from him wifh'd death, hadft thou been

    He that with thine fhall weigh good David's deeds,
Shall find his paffion nor his love exceeds:
He curs'd the mountains where his brave friend dy'd,
But let falfe Ziba with his heir divide;   30
Where thy immortal love to thy bleft friends,
Like that of Heav'n, upon their feed defcends.
Such huge extremes inhabit thy great mind,
God-like, unmov'd, and yet, like woman, kind!

    * Achilles.   † Timanthes.   ‡ Cypariffus.

Which of the ancient poets had not brought 35
Our Charles's pedigree from Heav'n, and taught
How some bright dame, comprefs'd by mighty Jove,
Produc'd this mix'd Divinity and Love? 38

III.

ON THE

TAKING OF SALLE.

Of Jafon, Thefeus, and fuch worthies old,
Light feem the tales Antiquity has told :
Such beafts and monfters as their force oppreft,
Some places only, and fome times, infeft.
Salle, that fcorn'd all pow'r and laws of men, 5
Goods with their owners hurrying to their den,
And future ages threat'ning with a rude
And favage race, fucceffively renew'd ;
Their king defpifing with rebellious pride,
And foes profeft to all the world befide ; 10
This peft of mankind gives our hero fame,
And thro' th' obliged world dilates his name.
  The Prophet once to cruel Agag faid,
As thy fierce fword has mothers childlefs made,
So fhall the fword make thine ; and with that word 15
He hew'd the man in pieces with his fword :
Juft Charles like meafure has return'd to thefe
Whofe Pagan hands had ftain'd the troubled feas ;
With fhips they made the fpoiled merchant mourn ;
With fhips their city and themfelves are torn. 20

One fquadron of our winged caftles fent,
O'erthrew their fort, and all their navy rent;
For not content the dangers to increafe,
And act the part of tempefts in the feas,
Like hungry wolves, thofe pirate from our fhore 25
Whole flocks of fheep, and ravifh'd cattle bore.
Safely they might on other nations prey,
Fools to provoke the Sov'reign of the fea !
Mad Cacus fo, whom like ill fate perfuades,
The herd of fair Alemena's feed invades,   30
Who for revenge, and mortals' glad relief,
Sack'd the dark cave, and crufh'd that horrid thief.
. Morocco's monarch, wondering at this fact,
Save that his prefence his affairs exact,
Had come in perfon to have feen and known   35
The injur'd world's revenger and his own.
Hither he fends the chief among his peers,
Who in his bark proportion'd prefents bears;
To the renown'd for piety and force,
Poor captives manumis'd, and matchlefs horfe.   40

IV.

UPON HIS MAJESTY'S

REPAIRING OF ST. PAUL'S.

THAT fhipwreck'd veffel which th' Apoftle bore,
Scarce fuffer'd more upon Melita's fhore,

Than did his temple in the fea of time,
Our nation's glory, and our nation's crime.
When the firſt Monarch * of this happy iſle, 5
Mov'd with the ruin of fo brave a pile,
This work of coſt and piety begun,
To be accompliſh'd by his glorious fon,
Who all that came within the ample thought
Of his wife fire has to perfection brought ; 10
He, like Amphion, makes thofe quarries leap
Into fair figures from a confus'd heap;
For in his art of regiment is found
A pow'r like that of harmony in found.

Thofe antique minſtrels fure wereCharles-like kings,
Cities their lutes, and fubjects' hearts their ſtrings, 16
On which with fo divine a hand they ſtrook,
Confent of motion from their breath they took :
So all our minds with his confpire to grace
The Gentiles' great apoſtle, and deface 20
Thofe ſtate-obfcuring ſhades, that like a chain
Seem'd to confine and fetter him again;
Which the glad faint ſhakes off at his command,
As once the viper from his facred hand :
So joys the aged oak, when we divide 25
The creeping ivy from his injur'd fide.

Ambition rather would affect the fame
Of fome new ſtructure, to have borne her name.
Two diſtant virtues in one act we find,
The modeſty and greatnefs of his mind; 30

* King James I.

Which not content to be above the rage,
And injury of all-impairing age,
In its own worth fecure, doth higher climb,
And things half fwallowed from the jaws of time
Reduce; an earneft of his grand defign,   35
To frame no new church, but the old refine;
Which, fpoufe-like, may with comely grace command,
More than by force of argument or hand.
For doubtful reafon few can apprehend,
And **war** brings ruin where it fhould **amend**;   40
But beauty, with a bloodlefs conqueft, finds
A welcome fov'reignty in rudeft minds.

    Not ought which Sheba's wond'ring queen beheld
Amongft the works of Solomon, excell'd
His fhips and building; emblems of a heart   45
Large both in magnanimity and art.

    While the propitious heav'ns this work attend,
Long-wanted fhowers they forget to fend;
As if they meant to make it underftood
Of more importance than our vital food.   50

    The fun, which rifeth to falute the quire
Already finifh'd, fetting fhall admire
How private bounty could fo far extend:
The King built all, but Charles the weftern end.
So proud a fabric to devotion giv'n,   55
At once it threatens and obliges heav'n!

    Laomedon, that had the gods in pay,
Neptune, with him that rules the facred day *,

*Apollo.

Could no such structure raise: Troy wall'd so high,
Th'Atrides might as well have forc'd the sky. 60
    Glad, tho' amazed, are our neighbour kings,
To see such pow'r employ'd in peaceful things:
They list not urge it to the dreadful field;
The task is easier to destroy than build. 64

        ----- Sic gratia regum
        Picriis tentata modis.----   Hor.

V.

OF THE QUEEN.

The lark, that shuns on lofty boughs to build
Her humble nest, lies silent in the field;
But if (the promise of a cloudless day)
Aurora smiling bids her rise and play,
Then strait she shews 'twas not for want of voice, 5
Or pow'r to climb, she made so low a choice;
Singing she mounts; her airy wings are stretch'd
Tow'rds heav'n, as if from heav'n her note she fetch'd.

    So we, retiring from the busy throng,
Use to restrain th' ambition of our song; 10
But since the light which now informs our age
Breaks from the court, indulgent to her rage,
Thither my Muse, like bold Prometheus, flies,
To light her torch at Gloriana's eyes.

    Those sov'reign beams which heal the wounded soul,
And all our cares, but once beheld, controul! 16

There the poor lover, that has long endur'd
Some proud nymph's fcorn, of his fond paffion cur'd,
Fares like the man who firft upon the ground
A glow-worm fpy'd, fuppofing he had found   20
A moving diamond, a breathing ftone;
For life it had, and like thofe jewels fhone;
He held it dear, 'till by the fpringing day
Inform'd, he threw the worthlefs worm away.

    She faves the lover, as we gangrenes ftay,   25
By cutting hope, like a lopp'd limb, away:
This makes her bleeding patients to accufe
High Heav'n, and thefe expoftulations ufe:
" Could Nature then no private woman grace,
" Whom we might dare to love, with fuch a face, 30
" Such a complexion, and fo radiant eyes,
" Such lovely motion, and fuch fharp replics?
" Beyond our reach, and yet within our fight,
" What envious pow'r has plac'd this glorious light?"
    Thus in a ftarry night fond children cry   35
For the rich fpangles that adorn the fky,
Which, tho' they fhine for ever fixed there,
With light and influence relieve us here.
All her affections are to one inclin'd;
Her bounty and compaffion to mankind;   40
To whom, while fhe fo far extends her grace,
She makes but good the promife of her face:
For Mercy has, could Mercy's felf be feen,
No fweeter look than this propitious queen.

Such guard and comfort the diftreffed find   45
From her large pow'r, and from her larger mind,
That whom ill Fate would ruin it prefers,
For all the miferable are made her's.
So the fair tree whereon the eagle builds,
Poor fheep from tempefts, and their fhepherds, fhields:
The royal bird poffeffes all the boughs,   5I
But fhade and fhelter to the flock allows.

   Joy of our age, and fafety of the next!
For which fo oft' thy fertile womb is vext;
Nobly contented, for the public good,   55
To wafte thy fpirits and diffufe thy blood,
What vaft hopes may thefe iflands entertain,
Where monarchs, thus defcended, are to reign?
Led by commanders of fo fair a line,
Our feas no longer fhall our power confine.   6o

   A brave romance who would exactly frame,
Firft brings his knight from fome immortal dame,
And then a weapon and a flaming fhield,
Bright as his mother's eyes, he makes him wield.
None might the mother of Achilles be,   65
But the fair pearl and glory of the fea *:
The man to whom great Maro gives fuch fame †,
From the high bed of heav'nly Venus came;
And our next Charles, whom all the ftars defign
Like wonders to accomplifh, fprings from thine. 70

---

* Thetis.   † Aeneas.

VI.

THE APOLOGY OF SLEEP,

For not approaching the lady who can do any thing but
sleep when she pleaseth.

My charge it is those breaches to repair
Which Nature takes from sorrow, toil, and care:
Rest to the limbs, and quiet I confer
On troubled minds; but nought can add to her   4
Whom Heav'n, and her transcendent thoughts have
Above those ills which wretched mortals taste. [plac'd
  Bright as the deathless gods, and happy, she
From all that may infringe delight is free:
Love at her royal feet his quiver lays,
And not his mother with more haste obeys.   10
Such real pleasures, such true joys suspense,
What dream can I present to recompense?
  Should I with lightning fill her awful hand,
And make the clouds seem all at her command;
Or place her in Olympus' top, a guest   15
Among th' immortals, who with nectar feast,
That pow'r wou'd seem, that entertainment, short
Of the true splendour of her present court,
Where all the joys, and all the glories, are
Of three great kingdoms, sever'd from the care.   20
I, that of fumes and humid vapours made,
Ascending, do the seat of sense invade,

3

No cloud in fo ferene a manfion find,
To overcaft her ever-fhining mind,
Which holds refemblance with thofe fpotlefs fkies, 25
Where flowing Nilus want of rain fupplies;
That cryftal heav'n, where Phœbus never fhrouds
His golden beams, nor wraps his face in clouds.
But what fo hard which numbers cannot force?
So ftoops the moon, and rivers change their courfe. 30
The bold Mæonian * made me dare to fteep
Jove's dreadful temples in the dew of fleep;
And fince the Mufes do invoke my pow'r,
I fhall no more decline that facred bow'r
Where Gloriana their great miftrefs lies,   35
But gently taming thofe victorious eyes,
Charm all her fenfes, till the joyful fun
Without a rival half his courfe has run;
Who, while my hand that fairer light confines,
May boaft himfelf the brighteft thing that fhines. 40

VII.

PUERPERIUM.

You gods that have the pow'r
To trouble and compofe
All that's beneath **your** bow'r,
Calm filence on the feas, on earth impofe.

* Homer.

Fair Venus! in thy foft arms　　　　　　　　5
The God of Rage confine;
For thy whifpers are the charms
Which only can divert his fierce defign.

What tho' he frown, and to tumult do incline?
Thou the flame　　　　　　　　　　　10
Kindled in his breaft canft tame
With that fnow which unmelted lies on thine.

Great Goddefs! give this thy facred ifland reft;
Make heav'n fmile,
That no ftorm difturb us while　　　　　15
Thy chief care, our halcyon, builds her neft.

Great Gloriana! fair Gloriana!
Bright as high heav'n is, and fertile as earth,
Whofe beauty relieves us,
Whofe royal bed gives us　　　　　　　20
Both glory and peace,
Our prefent joy, and all our hopes increafe.　　22

VIII.

THE COUNTESS OF CARLISLE

IN MOURNING.

WHEN from black clouds no part of fky is clear,
But juft fo much as lets the fun appear,
Heav'n then would feem thy image, and reflect
Thofe fable veftments and that bright afpect.

A spark of virtue by the deepest shade   5
Of sad adversity is fairer made;
Nor less advantage doth thy beauty get,
A Venus rising from a sea of jet!
Such was th' appearance of new-formed Light,
While yet it struggled with eternal Night.   10
Then mourn no more, lest thou admit increase
Of glory by thy noble Lord's decease.
We find not that the laughter-loving dame *
Mourn'd for Anchises; 'twas enough she came
To grace the mortal with her deathless bed,   15
And that his living eyes such beauty fed:
Had she been there, untimely joy thro' all
Men's hearts diffus'd, had marr'd the funeral.
Those eyes were made to banish grief: as well
Bright Phœbus might affect in shades to dwell,   20
As they to put on sorrow: nothing stands,
But pow'r to grieve, exempt from thy commands.
If thou lament, thou must do so alone;
Grief in thy presence can lay hold on none.
Yet still persist the memory to love   25
Of that great Mercury of our mighty Jove,
Who, by the pow'r of his inchanting tongue,
Swords from the hands of threat'ning monarchs wrung.
War he prevented, or soon made it cease,
Instructing princes in the arts of peace;   30
Such as made Sheba's curious queen resort
To the large-hearted Hebrew's † famous court.

* Venus.   † Solomon.   G ij

Had Homer sat amongst his wond'ring guests,
He might have learn'd, at those stupendous feasts,
With greater bounty, and more sacred state,   35
The banquets of the gods to celebrate.
But, oh! what elocution might he use,
What potent charms, that could so soon infuse
His absent master's love into the heart
Of Henrietta! forcing her to part   40
From her lov'd brother, country, and the sun,
And, like Camilla, o'er the waves to run
Into his arms? while the Parisian dames
Mourn for the ravish'd glory; at her flames
No less amaz'd than the amazed stars,   45
When the bold charmer of Thessalia wars
With Heav'n itself, and numbers does repeat,
Which call descending Cynthia from her seat.   48

IX.

In answer to one who writ a libel against

THE COUNTESS OF CARLISLE.

WHAT fury has provok'd thy wit to dare,
With Diomede, to wound the Queen of Love?
Thy mistress' envy, or thine own despair?
Not the just Pallas in thy breast did move
So blind a rage, with such a diff'rent fate;   5
He honour won where thou hast purchas'd hate.

She gave affiftance to his Trojan foe;
Thou, that without a rival thou may'ft love,
Doft to the beauty of this Lady owe,
While after her the gazing world does move.　10
Canft thou not be content to love alone?
Or is thy miftrefs not content with one?

Haft thou not read of Fairy Arthur's fhield,
Which but difclos'd amaz'd the weaker eyes
Of proudeft foes, and won the doubtful field?　15
So fhall thy rebel wit become her prize.
Should thy Iambics fwell into a book,
All were confuted with one radiant look.

Heav'n he oblig'd that plac'd her in the fkies;
Rewarding Phœbus for infpiring fo　20
His noble brain, by likening to thofe eyes
His joyful beams; but Phœbus is thy foe,
And neither aids thy fancy nor thy fight,
So ill thou rhym'ft againft fo fair a light.　24

X.

OF HER CHAMBER.

They tafte of death that do at heav'n arrive,
But we this paradife approach alive.
Inftead of Death, the dart of Love does ftrike,
And renders all within thefe walls alike.

G iij

The high in titles, and the shepherd, here   5
Forgets his greatness, and forgets his fear.
All stand amaz'd, and gazing on the fair,
Lose thought of what themselves or others are:
Ambition lose, and have no other scope,
Save Carlisle's favour, to employ their hope.   10
The Thracian * could (tho' all those tales were true
The bold Greeks tell) no greater wonders do:
Before his feet so sheep and lions lay,
Fearless and wrathless while they heard him play.
The gay, the wise, the gallant, and the grave,   15
Subdu'd alike, all but one passion have:
No worthy mind but finds in her's there is
Something proportion'd to the rule of his:
While she with cheerful, but impartial grace,
(Born for no one, but to delight the race   20
Of men) like Phœbus so divides her light,
And warms us, that she stoops not from her height. 22

XI.

ON MY

LADY DOROTHY SIDNEY'S PICTURE.

Such was Philoclea, and such Dorus' † flame!
The matchless Sidney ‡, that immortal frame
Of perfect beauty, on two pillars plac'd,
Not his high fancy could one pattern, grac'd

* Orpheus.   † Pamela.   ‡ Sir Philip Sidney.

With such extremes of excellence, compose,   5
Wonders so diftant in one face difclofe!
Such cheerful modefty, fuch humble ftate,
Moves certain love, but with as doubtful fate
As when, beyond our greedy reach, we fee
Inviting fruit on too fublime a tree.   10
All the rich flow'rs thro' his Arcadia found,
Amaz'd we fee in this one garland bound.
Had but this copy (which the artift took
From the fair picture of that noble book)
Stood at Kalander's, the brave friends * had jarr'd, 15
And, rivals made, th' enfuing ftory marr'd.
Juft Nature, firft inftructed by his thought,
In his own houfe thus practis'd what he taught :
This glorious piece tranfcends what he could think,
So much his blood is nobler than his ink!   20

XII.

AT PENSHURST.

Had Dorothea liv'd when mortals made
Choice of their deities, this facred fhade
Had held an altar to her pow'r that gave
The peace and glory which thefe alleys have;
Embroider'd fo with flowers where fhe ftood,   5
That it became a garden of a wood.

* Pyrocles and Mufidorus.

Her prefence has fuch more than human grace,
That it can civilize the rudeft place;
And beauty too, and order, can impart,
Where Nature ne'er intended it, nor art.   10
The plants acknowledge this, and her admire,
No lefs than thofe of old did Orpheus' lyre.
If fhe fit down, with tops all tow'rds her bow'd,
They round about her into arbours crowd;
Or if fhe walk, in even ranks they ftand,   15
Like fome well-marfhall'd and obfequious band.
Amphion fo made ftones and timber leap
Into fair figures from a confus'd heap:
And in the fymmetry' of her parts is found
A pow'r like that of harmony in found.   20
    Ye lofty Beeches! tell this matchlefs dame,
That if together ye fed all one flame,
It could not equalize the hundredth part
Of what her eyes have kindled in my heart!——
Go, Boy, and carve this paffion on the bark   25
Of yonder tree, which ftands the facred mark
Of noble Sidney's birth; when fuch benign,
Such more than mortal-making ftars did fhine,
That there they cannot but for ever prove
The monument and pledge of humble love;   30
His humble love whofe hope fhall ne'er rife higher,
Than for a pardon that he dares admire.   32

XIII.

OF THE LADY

WHO CAN SLEEP WHEN SHE PLEASES.

No wonder Sleep from careful lovers flies,
To bathe himfelf in Sacharissa's eyes.
As fair Astræa once from earth to heav'n,
By strife and loud impiety was driven;
So with our plaints offended, and our tears, 5
Wise Somnus to that paradife repairs;
Waits on her will, and wretches does forfake,
To court the nymph for whom thofe wretches wake.
More proud than Phœbus of his throne of gold,
Is the foft God thofe fofter limbs to hold; 10
Nor would exchange with Jove, to hide the fkies
In dark'ning clouds, the pow'r to clofe her eyes;
Eyes which fo far all other lights control,
They warm our mortal parts, but thefe our foul!
Let her free fpirit, whofe unconquer'd breaft 15
Holds fuch deep quiet and untroubled reft,
Know that tho' Venus and her fon fhould fpare
Her rebel heart, and never teach her care,
Yet Hymen may in force his vigils keep,
And for another's joy fufpend her fleep. 20

XIV

OF THE MISREPORT

OF HER BEING PAINTED.

As when a sort of wolves infest the night
With their wild howlings at fair Cynthia's light,
The noise may chase sweet slumber from our eyes,
But never reach the mistress of the skies;
So with the news of Sacharissa's wrongs,   5
Her vexed servants blame those envious tongues;
Call Love to witness that no painted fire
Can scorch men so, or kindle such desire;
While, unconcerned, she seems mov'd no more
With this new malice than our loves before;   10
But from the height of her great mind looks down
On both our passions without smile or frown.
So little care of what is done below
Hath the bright dame whom Heav'n affecteth so!
Paints her, 'tis true, with the same hand which spreads
Like glorious colours thro' the flow'ry meads,   16
When lavish Nature, with her best attire,
Clothes the gay spring, the season of desire.
Paints her, 'tis true, and does her cheek adorn
With the same art wherewith she paints the morn; 20
With the same art wherewith she gildeth so
Those painted clouds which form Thaumantias' bow. 22

XV.

OF HER PASSING

THROUGH A CROWD OF PEOPLE.

As in old chaos (heav'n with earth confus'd,
And stars with rocks together crush'd and bruis'd)
The sun his light no further could extend
Than the next hill, which on his shoulders lean'd;
So in this throng bright Sacharissa far'd,　　　5
Oppress'd by those who strove to be her guard;
As ships, tho' never so obsequious, fall
Foul in a tempest on their admiral.
A greater favour this disorder brought
Unto her servants than their awful thought　　　10
Durst entertain, when thus compell'd they prest
The yielding marble of her snowy breast.
While love insults, disguised in the cloud
And welcome force of that unruly crowd.
So th' amorous tree, while yet the air is calm,　　　15
Just distance keeps from his desired palm;
But when the wind her ravish'd branches throws
Into his arms, and mingles all their boughs,
Tho' loath he seems her tender leaves to press,
More loath he is that friendly storm should cease, 20
From whose rude bounty he the double use
At once receives, of pleasure and excuse.　　　22

XVI.

THE STORY OF

PHOEBUS AND DAPHNE

APPLIED.

THYRSIS, a youth of the inspired train,
Fair Sacharissa lov'd, but lov'd in vain:
Like Phœbus sung the no less am'rous boy;
Like Daphne she, as lovely, and as coy!
With numbers he the flying nymph pursues,   5
With numbers such as Phœbus' self might use!
Such is the chase when Love and Fancy leads,
O'er craggy mountains, and thro' flow'ry meads ;
Invok'd to testify the lover's care,
Or form some image of his cruel fair.   10
Urg'd with his fury, like a wounded deer,
O'er these he fled ; and now approaching near,
Had reach'd the nymph with his harmonious lay,
Whom all his charms could not incline to stay.
Yet what he sung in his immortal strain,   15
Tho' unsuccessful, was not sung in vain :
All but the nymph that should redress his wrong,
Attend his passion, and approve his song.
Like Phœbus thus, acquiring unsought praise,
He catch'd at love, and fill'd his arms with bays.   20

XVII.

FABULA PHOEBI ET DAPHNES.

Arcadiæ juvenis Thyrsis, Phœbique sacerdos,
Ingenti frustra Sachariffæ ardebat amore.
Haud Deus ipse olim Daphni majora canebat;
Nec fuit asperior Daphne, nec pulchrior illâ:
Carminibus Phœbo dignis premit ille fugacem   5
Per rupes, per saxa, volans per florida vates
Pascua: formosam nunc his componere nympham,
Nunc illis crudelem insanâ mente solebat.
Audiit illa procul miserum, cytharamque sonantem;
Audiit, at nullis respexit mota querelis!   10
Ne tamen omnino caneret desertus, ad alta
Sidera perculsi referunt nova carmina montes.
Sic, non quæsitis cumulatus laudibus, olim
Elapsâ reperit Daphne sua laurea Phœbus   14

XVIII.

AT PENSHURST.

While in this park I sing, the list'ning deer
Attend my passion, and forget to fear.
When to the beeches I report my flame,
They bow their heads, as if they felt the same.
To gods appealing, when I reach their bow'rs   5
With loud complaints, they answer me in show'rs.

To thee a wild and cruel foul is giv'n,
More deaf than trees, and prouder than the heav'n!
Love's foe profefs'd! why doft thou falfely feign
Thyfelf a Sidney? from which noble ftrain   10
He fprung *, that could fo far exalt the name
Of Love, and warm our nation with his flame;
That all we can of love or high defire
Seems but the fmoke of am'rous Sidney's fire.
Nor call her mother who fo well does prove   15
One breaft may hold both chaftity and love.
Never can fhe, that fo exceeds the fpring
In joy and bounty, be fuppos'd to bring
One fo deftructive. To no human ftock
We owe this fierce unkindnefs, but the rock,   20
That cloven rock produc'd thee, by whofe fide
Nature, to recompenfe the fatal pride
Of fuch ftern beauty, plac'd thofe healing fprings †,
Which not more help than that deftruction brings.
Thy heart no ruder than the rugged ftone,   25
I might, like Orpheus, with my num'rous moan
Melt to compaffion: now my trait'rous fong
With thee confpires to do the finger wrong;
While thus I fuffer not myfelf to lofe
The memory of what augments my woes;   30
But with my own breath ftill foment the fire,
Which flames as high as fancy can afpire!

* Sir Philip Sidney.   † Tunbridge-Wells.

This laſt complaint th' indulgent ears did pierce
Of juſt Apollo, preſident of verſe ;
Highly concerned that the Muſe ſhould bring   35
Damage to one whom he had taught to ſing :
Thus he advis'd me : " On yon' aged tree
" Hang up thy lute, and hie thee to the ſea,
" That there with wonders thy diverted mind
" Some truce, at leaſt, may with this paſſion find." 40
Ah, cruel Nymph ! from whom her humble ſwain
Flies for relief unto the raging main,
And from the winds and tempeſts does expect
A milder fate than from her cold neglect !
Yet there he'll pray that the unkind may prove   45
Bleſt in her choice ; and vows this endleſs love
Springs from no hope of what ſhe can confer,
But from thoſe giftswhichHeav'n has heap'd on her. 48

XIX.

ON THE FRIENDSHIP BETWIXT

SACHARISSA AND AMORET.

TELL me, lovely, loving Pair !
Why ſo kind, and ſo ſevere ?
Why ſo careleſs of our care,
Only to yourſelves ſo dear ?

H ij

By this cunning change of hearts,
You the pow'r of Love control,
While the Boy's deluded darts
Can arrive at neither foul.

For in vain to either breaft
Still beguiled Love does come,
Where he finds a foreign gueft,
Neither of your hearts at home.

Debtors thus with like defign,
When they never mean to pay,
That they may the law decline,
To fome friend make all away.

Not the filver doves that fly,
Yok'd in Cytherea's car,
Not the wings that lift fo high,
And convey her fon fo far,

Are fo lovely, fweet, and fair,
Or do more ennoble love;
Are fo choicely match'd a pair,
Or with more confent do move.

XX.

A LA MALADE.

Ah, lovely Amoret! the care
Of all that know what's good or fair!
Is heav'n become our rival too?
Had the rich gifts conferr'd on you
So amply thence, the common end   5
Of giving lovers—to pretend?

Hence to this pining ficknefs (meant
To weary thee to a confent
Of leaving us) no pow'r is giv'n
Thy beauties to impair; for Heav'n   10
Solicits thee with fuch a care,
As rofes from their ftalks we tear,
When we would ftill preferve them new
And frefh as on the bufh they grew.

With fuch a grace you entertain,   15
And look with fuch contempt on pain,
That languifhing you conquer more,
And wound us deeper than before.
So lightnings which in ftorms appear
Scorch more than when the fkies are clear.   20

And as pale ficknefs does invade
Your frailer part, the breaches made
In that fair lodging, ftill more clear
Make the bright gueft, your foul, appear.

H iij

So nymphs o'er pathlefs mountains borne, 25
Their light robes by the brambles torn,
From their fair limbs, expofing new
And unknown beauties to the view
Of following gods, increafe their flame,
And hafte to catch the flying game. 30

XXI.

UPON THE DEATH

OF MY LADY RICH.

Mᴀʏ thofe already curs'd Effexian plains,
Where hafty death and pining ficknefs reigns,
Prove all a defert! and none there make ftay,
But favage beafts, or men as wild as they !
There the fair light which all our ifland grac'd, 5
Like Hero's taper in the window plac'd,
Soch fate from the malignant air did find,
As that expofed to the boift'rous wind.
   Ah, cruel Heav'n! to fnatch fo foon away
Her for whofe life, had we had time to pray, 10
With thoufand vows and tears we fhould have fought
That fad decree's fufpenfion to have wrought.
But we, alas, no whifper of her pain
Heard, till 'twas fin to wifh her here again.

That horrid word, at once, like lightning fpread, 15
Strook all our ears,——The Lady Rich is dead!
Heart-rending news! and dreadful to thofe few
Who her refemble, and her fteps purfue;
That Death fhould licenfe have to rage among
The fair, the wife, the virtuous, and the young! 20
   The Paphian Queen * from that fierce battle borne,
With gored hand, and veil fo rudely torn,
Like terror did among th' immortals breed,
Taught by her wound that goddeffes may bleed.
   All ftand amazed! but beyond the reft 25
Th' heroic dame † whofe happy womb fhe bleft,
Mov'd with juft grief, expoftulates with Heav'n,
Urging the promife to th' obfequious giv'n,
Of longer life; for ne'er was pious foul
More apt t' obey, more worthy to control. 30
A fkilful eye at once might read the race
Of Caledonian monarchs in her face,
And fweet humility: her look and mind
At once were lofty, and at once were kind.
There dwelt the fcorn of vice, and pity too, 35
For thofe that did what fhe difdain'd to do:
So gentle and fevere, that what was bad,
At once her hatred and her pardon had.
Gracious to all; but where her love was due,
So faft, fo faithful, loyal, and fo true, 40

* Venus.　　† Chriftian Countefs of Devonfhire,

That a bold hand as foon might hope to force
The rolling lights of heav'n as change her courfe.
   Some happy angel, that beholds her there,
Inftruct us to record what fhe was here!
And when this cloud of forrow's over-blown,   45
Thro' the wide world we'll make her graces known.
So frefh the wound is, and the grief fo vaft,
That all our art and pow'r of fpeech is wafte.
Here paffion fways, but there the Mufe fhall raife
Eternal monuments of louder praife.   50
   There our delight complying with her fame,
Shall have occafion to recite thy name,
Fair Sachariffa!——and now only fair!
To facred friendfhip we'll an altar rear,
(Such as the Romans did erect of old)   55
Where on a marble pillar fhall be told
The lovely paffion each to other bare,
With the refemblance of that matchlefs pair.
Narciffus to the thing for which he pin'd,
Was not more like than your's to her fair mind,   60
Save that fhe grac'd the fev'ral parts of life,
A fpotlefs virgin, and a faultlefs wife.
Such was the fweet converfe 'twixt her and you,
As that fhe holds with her affociates now.
   How falfe is Hope, and how regardlefs Fate,   65
That fuch a love fhould have fo fhort a date!
Lately I faw her fighing part from thee;
(Alas that that the laft farewell fhould be!)

So look'd Aſtræa, her remove deſign'd,
On thoſe diſtreſſed friends ſhe left behind. 70
Conſent in virtue knit your hearts ſo faſt,
That ſtill **the** knot, in ſpight of death, does laſt;
For as your tears, and ſorrow-wounded ſoul,
Prove well that on your part this bond is whole,
So **all** we know of what they do above, 75
Is that they happy are, and that they love.
Let dark oblivion, and the hollow grave,
Content themſelves our frailer thoughts to have:
Well choſen love is never taught to die,
But with our nobler part invades the ſky. 80
Then grieve no more that one ſo heav'nly ſhap'd
The crooked hand of trembling Age eſcap'd:
Rather, ſince we beheld her not decay,
But that ſhe vaniſh'd ſo entire away,
Her wondrous beauty and her goodneſs merit 85
We ſhould ſuppoſe that ſome propitious ſpirit
In that celeſtial form frequented here,
And is not dead, but ceaſes to appear. 88

XXII.

OF LOVE.

Aɴɢᴇʀ, in haſty words or blows,
Itſelf diſcharges on our foes;
And ſorrow, too, finds ſome relief
In tears, which wait upon our grief:

So ev'ry paffion, but fond love,   5
Unto its own redrefs does move;
But that alone the wretch inclines
To what prevents his own defigns;
Makes him lament, and figh, and weep,
Diforder'd, tremble, fawn, and creep;   10
Poftures which render him defpis'd,
Where he endeavours to be priz'd.
For women, (born to be controll'd)
Stoop to the forward and the bold;
Affect the haughty and the proud,   15
The gay, the frolic, and the loud.
Who firft the gen'rous fteed oppreft,
Not kneeling did falute the beaft;
But with high courage, life, and force,
Approaching, tam'd th' unruly horfe.   20
    Unwifely we the wifer Eaft
Pity, fuppofing them oppreft
With tyrants' force, whofe law is will,
By which they govern, fpoil, and kill:
Each nymph, but moderately fair,   25
Commands with no lefs rigour here.
Should fome brave **Turk**, that walks among
His twenty laffes, bright and young,
And beckons to the willing dame,
Preferr'd to quench his prefent flame,   30
Behold as many gallants here,
With modeft guife and filent fear,

All to one female idol bend,
While her high pride does scarce descend
To mark their follies, he would swear   35
That these her guard of eunuchs were,
And that a more majestic queen,
Or humbler slaves, he had not seen.

All this with indignation spoke,
In vain I struggled with the yoke   40
Of mighty Love: that conqu'ring look,
When next beheld, like lightning strook
My blasted soul, and made me bow
Lower than those I pity'd now.

So the tall stag, upon the brink   45
Of some smooth stream about to drink,
Surveying there his armed head,
With shame remembers that he fled
The scorned dogs, resolves to try
The combat next; but if their cry   50
Invades again his trembling ear,
He strait resumes his wonted care,
Leaves the untasted spring behind,
And, wing'd with fear, outflies the wind.   54

XXIII.

FOR DRINKING OF HEALTHS.

LET brutes and vegetals, that cannot think,
So far as drought and nature urges, drink;

A more indulgent miſtreſs guides our ſp'rits,
Reaſon, that dares beyond our appetites:
She would our care as well as thirſt redreſs,　　　5
And with divinity rewards exceſs.
Deſerted Ariadne, thus ſupply'd,
Did perjur'd Theſeus' cruelty deride:
Bacchus embrac'd, from her exalted thought
Baniſh'd the man, her paſſion, and his fault.　　　10
Bacchus and Phœbus are by Jove ally'd,
And each by other's timely heat ſupply'd:
All that the grapes owe to his rip'ning fires
Is paid in numbers which their juice inſpires.
Wine fills the veins, and healths are underſtood　15
To give our friends a title to our blood:
Who, naming me, doth warm his courage ſo,
Shews for my ſake what his bold hand would do.　18

XXIV.

OF MY LADY ISABELLA,

PLAYING ON THE LUTE.

Such moving ſounds from ſuch a careleſs touch!
So unconcern'd herſelf, and we ſo much!
What art is this, that with ſo little pains
Tranſports us thus, and o'er our ſpirits reigns?
The trembling ſtrings about her fingers crowd,　　5
And tell their joy for ev'ry kiſs aloud.

Small force there needs to make them tremble so;
Touch'd by that hand, who would not tremble too?
Here Love takes stand, and while she charms the ear,
Empties his quiver on the list'ning deer. 10
Music so softens and disarms the mind,
That not an arrow does resistance find.
Thus the fair tyrant celebrates the prize,
And acts herself the triumph of her eyes:
So Nero once, with harp in hand, survey'd
His flaming Rome, and as it burn'd he play'd. 16

XXV.

OF MRS. ARDEN.

Behold, and listen, while the fair
Breaks in sweet sounds the willing air,
And with her own breath fans the fire
Which her bright eyes do first inspire.
What reason can that love control, 5
Which more than one way courts the soul?
· So when a flash of lightning falls
On our abodes, the danger calls
For human aid, which hopes the flame
To conquer, tho' from heav'n it came; 10
But if the winds with that conspire,
Men strive not, but deplore the fire. 12

XXVI.

OF THE

MARRIAGE OF THE DWARFS.

DESIGN or Chance makes others wive,
But Nature did this match contrive :
Eve might as well have Adam fled,
As she deny'd her little bed
To him, for whom Heav'n seem'd to frame   5
And measure out this only dame.

Thrice happy is that humble pair,
Beneath the level of all care!
Over whose heads those arrows fly
Of sad distrust and jealousy;   10
Secured in as high extreme,
As if the world held none but them.
   To him the fairest nymphs do show
Like moving mountains top'd with snow;
And ev'ry man a Polypheme   15
Does to his Galatea seem :
None may presume her faith to prove;
He proffers death that proffers love.
   Ah, Chloris! that kind Nature thus
From all the world had sever'd us;   20
Creating for ourselves us two,
As Love has me for only you!   22

XXVII.

LOVE'S FAREWELL.

TREADING the path to nobler ends,
A long farewell to love I gave,
Refolv'd my country and my friends
All that remain'd of me fhould have.

And this refolve no mortal dame,   5
None but thofe eyes could have o'erthrown;
The nymph I dare not, need not name,
So high, fo like herfelf alone.

Thus the tall oak, which now afpires
Above the fear of private fires,   10
Grown and defign'd for nobler ufe,
Not to make warm, but build the houfe,
Tho' from our meaner flames fecure,
Muft that which falls from heav'n endure.   14

XXVIII.

FROM A CHILD.

MADAM, as in fome climes the warmer fun
Makes it full fummer e'er the fpring's begun,
And with ripe fruit the bending boughs can load,
Before our violets dare look abroad;

I ij

So meafure not by any **common ufe**   5
The early love your brighter eyes produce.
When lately your fair hand in woman's weed
Wrapp'd my glad head, I wifh'd me fo indeed,
That hafty time might never make me grow
Out of thofe favours you afford me now;   10
That I might ever fuch indulgence find,
And you not blufh, or think yourfelf too kind:
Who now, I fear, while I thefe joys exprefs,
Begin to think how you may make them lefs.
The found of love makes your foft heart afraid,   15
And guard itfelf, tho' but a child invade,
And innocently at your white breaft throw
A dart as white, a ball of new-fall'n fnow.   18

XXIX.

ON A GIRDLE.

THAT which her flender waift confin'd,
Shall now my joyful temples bind:
No monarch but would give his crown,
His arms might do what this has done.

   It was my heav'n's extremeft fphere,   5
The pale which held that lovely deer.
My joy, my grief, my hope, my love,
Did all within this circle move!

A narrow compaſs! and yet there
Dwelt all that's good, and all that's fair: 10
Give me but what this ribband bound,
Take all the reſt the ſun goes round.

XXX.

THE FALL.

See! how the willing earth gave way,
To take th' impreſſion where ſhe lay.
See! how the mould, as loath to leave
So ſweet a burden, ſtill doth cleave
Cloſe to the nymph's ſtain'd garment. Here   5
The coming ſpring would firſt appear,
And all this place with roſes ſtrow,
If buſy feet would let them grow.
    Here Venus ſmil'd to ſee blind Chance
Itſelf before her ſon advance,   10
And a fair image to preſent,
Of what the Boy ſo long had meant.
'Twas ſuch a chance as this made all
The world into this order fall;
Thus the firſt lovers, on the clay,   15
Of which they were compoſed, lay.
So in their prime, with equal grace,
Met the firſt patterns of our race.
    Then bluſh not, Fair! or on him frown,
Or wonder how you both came down;   20

But touch him, and he'll tremble strait;
How could he then support your weight?
How could the youth, alas! but bend,
When his whole heav'n upon him lean'd?
If ought by him amiss were done,
'Twas that he let you rise so soon.   26

XXXI.

OF SYLVIA.

Our sighs are heard; just Heav'n declares
The sense it has of lovers' cares:
She that so far the rest outshin'd,
Sylvia the fair, while she was kind,
As if her frowns impair'd her brow,   5
Seems only not unhandsome now.
So when the sky makes us endure
A storm, itself becomes obscure.

Hence 'tis that I conceal my flame,
Hiding from Flavia's self her name,   10
Lest she, provoking Heav'n, should prove
How it rewards neglected love.
Better a thousand such as I,
Their grief untold, should pine and die,
Than her bright morning, overcast   15
With sullen clouds, should be defac'd.   16

XXXII.

THE BUD.

Lately on yonder fwelling bufh,
Big with many a coming rofe,
This early bud began to blufh,
And did but half itfelf difclofe:
I pluck'd it tho' no better grown,   5
And now you fee how full 'tis blown.

Still as I did the leaves infpire,
With fuch a purple light they fhone,
As if they had been made of fire,
And fpreading fo, would flame anon.   10
All that was meant by air or fun,
To the young flow'r, my breath has done.

If our loofe breath fo much can do,
What may the fame in forms of love,
Of pureft love, and mufic too,   15
When Flavia it afpires to move?
When that which lifelefs buds perfuades
To wax more foft her youth invades?   18

XXXIII.

ON THE DISCOVERY

OF A LADY'S PAINTING.

Pygmalion's fate revers'd is mine;
His marble love took flesh and blood:
All that I worshipp'd as divine,
That beauty! now 'tis understood
Appears to have no more of life
Than that whereof he fram'd his wife.

As women yet, who apprehend
Some sudden cause of causeless fear,
Altho' that seeming cause take end,
And they behold no danger near,
A shaking thro' their limbs they find,
Like leaves saluted by the wind:

So tho' the beauty do appear
No beauty, which amaz'd me so;
Yet from my breast I cannot tear
The passion which from thence did grow;
Nor yet out of my fancy raze
The print of that suppos'd face.

A real beauty, tho' too near,
The fond Narciffus did admire :

I dote on that which is no where;
The fign of beauty feeds my fire.
No mortal flame was e'er fo cruel
As this, which thus furvives the fuel!			24

XXXIV.

OF LOVING AT FIRST SIGHT.

Not caring to obferve the wind,
Or the new fea explore,
Snatch'd from myfelf, how far behind
Already I behold the fhore!

May not a thoufand dangers fleep			5
In the fmooth bofom of this deep?
No: 'tis fo rocklefs and fo clear,
That the rich bottom does appear
Pav'd all with precious things; not torn
From fhipwreck'd veffels, but there borne.			10
(

Sweetnefs, truth, and ev'ry grace,
Which time and ufe are wont to teach,
The eye may in a moment reach,
And read diftinctly in her face.

Some other nymphs with colours faint,			15
And pencil flow, may Cupid paint,

And a weak heart in time deftroy;
She has a ftamp, and prints the Boy;
Can with a fingle look inflame
The coldeft breaft, the rudeft tame.

XXXV.

THE SELF-BANISHED.

It is not that I love you lefs,
Than when before your feet I lay;
But to prevent the fad increafe
Of hopelefs love, I keep away.

In vain, alas! for ev'ry thing
Which I have known belong to you,
Your form does to my fancy bring,
And makes my old wounds bleed anew.

Who in the fpring, from the new fun,
Already has a fever got,
Too late begins thofe fhafts to fhun,
Which Phœbus thro' his veins has fhot:

Too late he would the pain affwage,
And to thick fhadows does retire;
About with him he bears the rage,
And in his tainted blood the fire.

But vow'd I have, and never muſt
Your baniſh'd ſervant trouble you;
For if I break, you may miſtruſt
The vow I made—to love you too.   20

XXXVI.

THYRSIS, GALATEA.

THYRSIS.

As lately I on ſilver Thames did ride,
Sad Galatea on the bank I ſpy'd:
Such was her look as ſorrow taught to ſhine,
And thus ſhe grac'd me with a voice divine.   4
   GAL. You that can tune your ſounding ſtrings ſo well,
Of ladies' beauties, and of love to tell,
Once change your note, and let your lute report
The juſteſt grief that ever touch'd the Court.
   THYR. Fair nymph! I have in your delights no
Nor ought to be concerned in your care;   [ſhare,
Yet would I ſing if I your ſorrows knew,   11
And to my aid invoke no Muſe but you.
   GAL. Hear then, and let your ſong augment our
Which is ſo great as not to wiſh relief.   [grief,
   She that had all which Nature gives, or Chance,15
Whom Fortune join'd with Virtue to advance
To all the joys this iſland could afford,
The greateſt miſtreſs, and the kindeſt lord;

Who with the royal mixt her noble blood,
And in high grace with Gloriana stood;   20
Her bounty, sweetness, beauty, goodness, such,
That none e'er thought her happiness too much;
So well-inclin'd her favours to confer,
And kind to all, as Heav'n had been to her!
The virgin's part, the mother, and the wife,   25
So well she acted in this span of life,
That tho' few years (too few, alas!) she told,
She seem'd in all things but in beauty old.
As unripe fruit, whose verdant stalks do cleave
Close to the tree, which grieves no less to leave   30
The smiling pendent which adorns her so,
And until autumn on the bough should grow;
So seem'd her youthful soul not eas'ly forc'd,
Or from so fair, so sweet, a seat divorc'd:
Her fate at once did hasty seem and slow;   35
At once too cruel, and unwilling too.
   THYR. Under how hard a law are mortals born!
Whom now we envy, we anon must mourn:
What Heav'n sets highest, and seems most to prize,
Is soon removed from our wond'ring eyes!   40
But since the Sisters * did so soon untwine
So fair a thread, I'll strive to piece the line.
Vouchsafe, sad Nymph! to let me know the dame,
And to the Muses I'll commend her name:

* Parcae.

3

Make the wide country echo to your moan, 45
The lift'ning trees and favage mountains groan.
What rock's not moved when the death is fung
Of one fo good, fo lovely, and fo young?

GAL.'Twas Hamilton!—whom I had nam'd before,
But naming her, grief lets me fay no more 50

XXXVII.

ON THE HEAD OF A STAG.

So we fome antique hero's ftrength
Learn by his lance's weight and length;
As thefe vaft beams exprefs the beaft,
Whofe fhady brows alive they dreft.
Such game, while yet the world was new, 5
The mighty Nimrod did purfue.
What huntfman of our feeble race,
Or dogs, dare fuch a monfter chafe?
Refembling, with each blow he ftrikes,
The charge of a whole troop of pikes. 10
O fertile Head! which every year
Could fuch a crop of wonder bear!
The teeming earth did never bring,
So foon, fo hard, fo huge a thing;
Which might it never have been caft, 15
(Each year's growth added to the laft)
Thefe lofty branches had fupply'd
The earth's bold fons' prodigious pride:

Heav'n with thefe engines had been fcal'd,
When mountains heap'd on mountains fail'd.   20

XXXVIII.

THE MISER'S SPEECH.

IN A MASK.

BALLS of this metal flack'd At'lanta's pace,
And on the am'rous youth * beftow'd the race :
Venus, (the nymph's mind meafuring by her own)
Whom the rich fpoils of cities overthrown
Had proftrated to Mars, could well advife   5
Th' advent'rous lover how to gain the prize.
Nor lefs may Jupiter to gold afcribe,
For when he turn'd himfelf into a bribe,
Who can blame Danae, or the brazen tow'r,
That they withftood not that almighty fhow'r?   10
Never till then did love make Jove put on
A form more bright and nobler than his own;
Nor were it juft, would he refume that fhape,
That flack devotion fhould his thunder fcape.
'Twas not revenge for griev'd Apollo's wrong,   15
Thofe afs's ears on Midas' temples hung,
But fond repentance of his happy wifh,
Becaufe his meat grew metal like his difh.

* Hippomenes.

Would Bacchus blefs me fo, I'd conftant hold
Unto my wifh, and die creating gold.   20

XXXIX.

UPON BEN. JOHNSON.

Mirror of Poets! mirror of our age!
Which her whole face beholding on thy ftage,
Pleas'd and difpleas'd with her own faults, endures
A remedy like thofe whom mufic cures.
Thou haft alone thofe various inclinations   5
Which Nature gives to ages, fexes, nations;
So traced with thy all-refembling pen,
That whate'er cuftom has impos'd on men,
Or ill-got habit, (which deforms them fo,
That fcarce a brother can his brother know)   10
Is reprefented to the wond'ring eyes
Of all that fee or read thy Comedies.
Whoever in thofe glaffes looks, may find
The fpots return'd, or graces, of his mind;
And by the help of fo divine an art,   15
At leifure view and drefs his nobler part.
Narciffus, cozen'd by that flatt'ring well,
Which nothing could but of his beauty tell,
Had here, difcov'ring the deform'd eftate
Of his fond mind, preferv'd himfelf with hate.   20
But virtue too, as well as vice, is clad
In flefh and blood fo well, that Plato had

Beheld, what his high fancy once embrac'd,
Virtue with colours, fpeech, and motion grac'd.
The fundry poftures of thy copious Mufe   25
Who would exprefs, a thoufand tongues muft ufe,
Whofe fate's no lefs peculiar than thy art;
For as thou couldft all characters impart,
So none could render thine, which ftill efcapes,
Like Proteus, in variety of fhapes;   30
Who was nor this nor that; but all we find,
And all we can imagine, in mankind.   32

XL.

ON MR. JOHN FLETCHER'S PLAYS.

Fletcher! to thee we do not only owe
All thefe good plays, but thofe of others too:
Thy wit repeated does fupport the ftage,
Credits the laft, and entertains this age.
No worthies, form'd by any Mufe but thine,   5
Could purchafe robes to make themfelves fo fine.

What brave commander is not proud to fee
Thy brave Melantius in his gallantry?
Our greateft ladies love to fee their fcorn
Outdone by thine, in what themfelves have worn: 10
Th' impatient widow, ere the year be done,
Sees thy Afpafia weeping in her gown.
I never yet the tragic ftrain affay'd,
Deterr'd by that inimitable maid *;

* The Maid's Tragedy.

And when I venture at the comic ftyle,   15
Thy Scornful Lady feems to mock my toil.

    Thus has thy Mufe at once improv'd and marr'd
Our fport in plays, by rend'ring it too hard!
So when a fort of lufty fhepherds throw
The bar by turns, and none the reft outgo   20
So far, but that the beft are meas'ring cafts,
Their emulation and their paftime lafts;
But if fome brawny yeoman of the **guard**
Step in, and tofs the axletree a yard
Or more beyond the furtheft mark, the reft
Defpairing ftand, their fport is at the beft.   26

XLI.

VERSES TO

DR. GEORGE ROGERS*,

On his taking the degree of Doctor in Phyfic at Padua, in the year 1664.

WHEN as of old the earth's bold children ftrove,
With hills on hills, to fcale the throne of Jove,

---

* This little poem (which is now firft inferted among Waller's Works) was printed, together with feveral others on the fame occafion, by Dr. Rogers, alone with his inaugural exercife at Padua, and afterwards in the fame manner republifhed by him at London, together with his Harveian oration before the College of Phyficians, in the year 1682, while Mr. Waller was yet living.
    Though the above verfes were firft printed in 1664, they feem to have been written before the Reftoration, as appears from the lines toward the conclufion.

Pallas and Mars ſtood by their ſov'reign's ſide,
And their bright arms in his defence employ'd;
While the wiſe Phœbus, Hermes, and the reſt,   5
Who joy in peace, and love the Muſes beſt,
Deſcending from their ſo diſtempered ſeat,
Our groves and meadows choſe for their retreat.
There firſt Apollo try'd the various uſe
Of herbs, and learn'd the virtues of their juice,   10
And fram'd that art, to which who can pretend
A juſter title than our noble Friend?
Whom the like tempeſt drives from his abode,
And like employment entertains abroad.
This crowns him here, and in the bays ſo earn'd,   15
His country's honour is no leſs concern'd,
Since it appears not all the Engliſh rave,
To ruin bent; ſome ſtudy how to ſave:
And as Hippocrates did once extend
His ſacred art, whole cities to amend;   20
So we, brave Friend! ſuppoſe that thy great ſkill,
Thy gentle mind, and fair example, will,
At thy return, reclaim our frantic iſle,
Their ſpirits calm, and peace again ſhall ſmile.   24

                    EDM. WALLER, Anglus.
                 Patavij, typis Pauli Frambotti.

XLII.

CHLORIS AND HYLAS.

MADE TO A SARABAND.

CHLORIS.

HYLAS, oh Hylas! why fit we mute,
Now that each bird faluteth the fpring?
Wind up the flacken'd ftrings of thy lute,
Never canft thou want matter to fing;
For love thy breaft does fill with fuch a fire,   5
That whatfoe'er is fair moves thy defire.

   HYL. Sweeteft! you know the fweeteft of things
Of various flow'rs the bees do compofe;
Yet no particular tafte it brings
Of violet, woodbine, pink, or rofe: 10
So love the refult is of all the graces
Which flow from a thoufand feveral faces.

   CHLO. Hylas! the birds which chant in this grove,
Could we but know the language they ufe,
They would inftruct us better in love,   15
And reprehend thy inconftant Mufe;
For love their breafts does fill with fuch a fire,
That what they once do chufe, bounds their defire.

   HYL. Chloris! this change the birds do approve,
Which the warm feafon hither does bring;   20
Time from yourfelf does further remove
You than the winter from the gay fpring:

She that like lightning fhin'd while her face lafted,
The oak now refembles which lightning hath blafted.

XLIII.

IN ANSWER OF

SIR JOHN SUCKLING'S VERSES.

CON.

STAY here, fond Youth! and afk no more; be wife;
Knowing too much long fince loft Paradife.
   PRO. And by your knowledge we fhould be bereft
Of all that paradife which yet is left.
     CON. The virtuous joys thou haft, thou wouldft
        fhould ftill   5
Laft in their pride ; and wouldft not take it ill
If rudely, from fweet dreams, and for a toy,
Thou wak'd : he wakes himfelf that does enjoy.
   PRO. How can the joy or hope which you allow
Be ftyled virtuous, and the end not fo?   10
Talk in your fleep, and fhadows ftill admire!
'Tis true, he wakes that feels this real fire;
But—to fleep better; for whoe'er drinks deep
Of this Nepenthe, rocks himfelf afleep.
    CON. Fruition adds no new wealth but deftroys, 15
And while it pleafeth much, yet ftill it cloys.
Who thinks he fhould be happier made for that,
As reas'nably might hope he might grow fat

By eating to a furfeit : this once paft,
What relifhes? ev'n kiffes lofe their tafte.   20

   PRO. Bleffings may be repeated while they cloy;
But fhall we ftarve, 'caufe furfeitings deftroy?
And if fruition did the tafte impair
Of kiffes, why fhould yonder happy pair,
Whofe joys juft Hymen warrants all the night,   25
Confume the day, too, in this lefs delight?

   CON. Urge not 'tis neceffary; alas! we know
The homelieft thing that mankind does is fo.
The world is of a large extent we fee,
And muft be peopled; children there muft be :—— 30
So muft bread too ; but fince there are enough
Born to that drudgery, what need we plough?

   PRO. I need not plough, fince what the ftooping hinc
Gets of my pregnant land muft all be mine :
But in this nobler tillage 'tis not fo;   35
For when Anchifes did fair Venus know,
What int'reft had poor Vulcan in the boy,
Famous Æneas, or the prefent joy ?

   CON. Women enjoy'd, whate'er before they've been,
Are like romances read, or fcenes once feen :   40
Fruition dulls or fpoils the play much more
Than if one read or knew the plot before.

   PRO. Plays and romances read and feen, do fall
In our opinions; yet not feen at all,
Whom would they pleafe? To an heroic tale   45
Would you not liften, left it fhould grow ftale?

CON. 'Tis expectation makes a blessing dear;
Heav'n were not heav'n if we knew what it were.

PRO. If 'twere not heav'n if we knew what it were,
'Twould not be heav'n to those that now are there. 50

CON. And as in prospects we are there pleas'd most,
Where something keeps the eye from being lost,
And leaves us room to guess; so here restraint
Holds up delight, that with excess would faint.

PRO. Restraint preserves the pleasure we have got,
But he ne'er has it that enjoys it not.   56
In goodly prospects who contracts the space,
Or takes not all the bounty of the place?
We wish remov'd what standeth in our light,
And Nature blame for limiting our sight;   60
Where you stand wisely winking, that the view
Of the fair prospect may be always new.

CON. They who know all the wealth they have are
He's only rich that cannot tell his store.   [poor;

PRO. Not he that knows the wealth he has is poor,
But he that dares not touch nor use his store.   66

XLIV.

AN APOLOGY

FOR HAVING LOVED BEFORE.

THEY that never had the use
Of the grape's surprising juice,

To the firſt delicious cup
All their reaſon render up;
Neither do nor care to know   5
Whether it be beſt or no.

So they that are to love inclin'd,
Sway'd by chance, not choice, or art,
To the firſt that's fair or kind,
Make a preſent of their heart :   10
It is not ſhe that firſt we love,
But whom dying we approve.

To man, that as in th' ev'ning made,
Stars gave the firſt delight,
Admiring, in the gloomy ſhade,   15
Thoſe little drops of light :
Then at Aurora, whoſe fair hand
Remov'd them from the ſkies,
He gazing tow'rd the eaſt did ſtand,
She entertain'd his eyes.   20

But when the bright ſun did appear,
All thoſe he 'gan deſpiſe ;
His wonder was determin'd there,
And could no higher riſe.
He neither might, nor wiſh'd to know   25
A more refulgent light :
For that (as mine your beauties now)
Employ'd his utmoſt ſight,   28

XLV.

THE NIGHT-PIECE:

OR, A PICTURE DRAWN IN THE DARK.

DARKNESS, which faireſt nymphs diſarms,
Defends us ill from Mira's charms:
Mira can lay her beauty by,
Take no advantage of the eye,
Quit all that Lely's art can take,   5
And yet a thouſand captives make.

  Her ſpeech is grac'd with ſweeter ſound
Than in another's ſong is found;
And all her well-plac'd words are darts,
Which need no light to reach our hearts.   10

  As the bright ſtars and Milky Way,
Shew'd by the night, are hid by day;
So we, in that accompliſh'd mind,
Help'd by the night, new graces find,
Which by the ſplendour of her view,   15
Dazzled before, we never knew.

  While we converſe with her, we mark
No want of day, nor think it dark:
Her ſhining image is a light
Fix'd in our hearts, and conquers night.   20

  Like jewels to advantage ſet,
Her beauty by the ſhade does get:

   2

There blushes, frowns, and cold disdain,
All that our passion might restrain,
Is hid, and our indulgent mind   25
Presents the fair idea kind.

   Yet, friended by the night, we dare
Only in whispers tell our care:
He that on her his bold hand lays,
With Cupid's pointed arrows plays;   30
They with a touch, (they are so keen!)
Wound us unshot, and she unseen.

   All near approaches threaten death;
We may be shipwreck'd by her breath:
Love, favour'd once with that sweet gale,   35
Doubles his haste, and fills his sail,
Till he arrive where she must prove
The haven or the rock of love.

   So we th'Arabian coast do know
At distance, when the spices blow;   40
By the rich odour taught to steer,
Tho' neither day nor stars appear,   42

XLVI.

PART OF THE FOURTH BOOK OF

VIRGIL'S ÆNEIS

TRANSLATED.

Beginning at V. 437.
• • • • Talefque miferrima fletus
Fertque refertque foror. • • • •
And ending with
Adnixi torquent fpumas, et caerula verrunt. V. 583.

ALL this her weeping fifter * does repeat
To the ftern man †, whom nothing could entreat;
Loft were her prayers, and fruitlefs were her tears!
Fate and great Jove had ftopp'd his gentle ears.
As when loud winds a well-grown oak would rend   5
Up by the roots, this way and that they bend
His reeling trunk, and with a boift'rous found
Scatter his leaves, and ftrew them on the ground,
He fixed ftands; as deep his roots doth lie
Down to the centre, as his top is high: 10
No lefs on ev'ry fide the hero preft,
Feels love and pity fhake his noble breaft,
And down his cheeks tho' fruitlet's tears do roll,
Unmov'd remains the purpofe of his foul.
Then Dido, urged with approaching fate,   15
Begins the light of cruel Heav'n to hate.

* Anna.   † Aeneas.

Her refolution to difpatch and die,
Confirm'd by many a horrid prodigy !
The water, confecrate for facrifice,
Appears all black to her amazed eyes;   20
The wine to putrid blood converted flows,
Which from her none, not her own fifter, knows.
Befides there ftood, as facred to her lord *,
A marble temple which fhe much ador'd,
With fnowy fleeces and frefh garlands crown'd; 25
Hence ev'ry night proceeds a dreadful found;
Her hufband's voice invites her to his tomb,
And difmal owls prefage the ills to come.
Befides, the prophefies of wizards old
Increas'd her terror, and her fall foretold: 30
Scorn'd and deferted to herfelf fhe feems,
And finds Æneas cruel in her dreams.
  So to mad Pentheus double Thebes appears,
And furies howl in his diftemper'd ears.
Oreftes fo, with like diftraction toft,   35
Is made to fly his mother's angry ghoft.
  Now grief and fury to their height arrive ;
Death fhe decrees, and thus does it contrive.
Her grieved fifter, with a cheerful grace,
(Hope well diffembled fhining in her face)   40
She thus deceives. Dear Sifter! let us prove
The cure I have invented for my love.   42

* Sichaeus.

L ij

Beyond the land of Ethiopia lies
The place where Atlas does support the skies;
Hence came an old magician, that did keep   45
Th' Hesperian fruit, and made the dragon sleep:
Her potent charms do troubled souls relieve,
And, where she lists, makes calmest minds to grieve:
The course of rivers, and of heav'n, can stop,
And call trees down from th' airy mountain's top. 50
Witness, ye Gods! and thou, my dearest part!
How loath I am to tempt this guilty art.
Erect a pile, and on it let us place
That bed where I my ruin did embrace!
With all the reliques of our impious guest,   55
Arms, spoils, and presents, let the pile be drest;
(The knowing woman thus prescribes) that we
May rase the man out of our memory.

   Thus speaks the Queen, but hides the fatal **end**
For which she doth those sacred rites pretend.   60
Nor worse effects of grief her sister thought
Would follow, than Sichæus' murder wrought;
Therefore obeys her: and now, heaped high
The cloven oaks and lofty pines do lie;
Hung all with wreaths and flowr'y garlands round, 65
So by herself was her own fun'ral crown'd!
Upon the top the Trojan's image lies,
And his sharp sword, wherewith anon she dies.
They by the altar stand, while with loose hair
The magic prophetess begins her pray'r: 70

On Chaos, Erebus, and all the gods,
Which in th' infernal fhades have their abodes,
She loudly calls, befprinkling all the room
With drops, fuppos'd from Lethe's lake to come.
She feeks the knot which on the forehead grows   75
Of new-foal'd colts, and herbs by moon-light mows.
A cake of leaven in her pious hands
Holds the devoted Queen, and barefoot ftands :
One tender foot was bare, the other fhod,
Her robe ungirt, invoking ev'ry god,   80
And ev'ry pow'r, if any be above,
Which takes regard of ill-requited love!

   Now was the time when weary mortals fleep
Their careful temples in the dew of fleep :
On feas, on earth, and all that in them dwell,   85
A death-like quiet and deep filence fell ;
But not on Dido! whofe untamed mind
Refus'd to be by facred night confin'd :
A double paffion in her breaft does move,
Love, and fierce anger for neglected love.   90
Thus fhe afflicts her foul: What fhall I do?
With fate inverted fhall I humbly woo?
And fome proud prince, in wild Numidia born,
Pray to accept me, and forget my fcorn?
Or fhall I with th' ungrateful Trojan go,   95
Quit all my ftate, and wait upon my foe?
Is not enough, by fad experience, known
The perjur'd race of falfe Laomedon?

With my Sidonians shall I give them chase,
Bands hardly forced from their native place?   100
No;—die! and let this sword thy fury tame;
Nought but thy blood can quench this guilty flame.

    Ah, Sister! vanquish'd with my passion, thou
Betray'dst me first, dispensing with my vow.
Had I been constant to Sichæus still,   105
And single liv'd, I had not known this ill!

    Such thoughts torment the Queen's enraged breast,
While the Dardanian does securely rest
In his tall ship, for sudden flight prepar'd,
To whom once more the son of Jove appear'd;   110
Thus seems to speak the youthful deity,
Voice, hair, and colour, all like Mercury.

    Fair Venus' seed! canst thou indulge thy sleep,
Nor better guard in such great danger keep?
Mad, by neglect to lose so fair a wind!   115
If here thy ships the purple morning find,
Thou shalt behold this hostile harbour shine
With a new fleet, and fires, to ruin thine:
She meditates revenge, resolv'd to die;
Weigh anchor quickly, and her fury fly.   120

    This said, the god in shades of night retir'd.
Amaz'd Æneas, with the warning fir'd,
Shakes off dull sleep, and rousing up his men,
Behold! the gods command our flight again.
Fall to your oars, and all your canvass spread: 125
What god soe'er that thus vouchsafes to lead,

We follow gladly, and thy will obey;
Affift us ftill, fmoothing our happy way,
And make the reft propitious!—With that word
He cuts the cable with his fhining fword: 130
'Thro' all the navy doth like ardour reign,
They quit the fhore, and rufh into the main:
Plac'd on their banks, the lufty Trojans fweep
Neptune's fmoothface,andcleavetheyieldingdeep. 134

XLVII.

on the

PICTURE OF A FAIR YOUTH,

TAKEN AFTER HE WAS DEAD.

As gather'd flowers, while their wounds are new,
Look gay and frefh, as on the ftalk they grew,
Torn from the root that nourifh'd them, a while
(Not taking notice of their fate) they fmile,
And in the hand which rudely pluck'd them fhow 5
Fairer than thofe that to their autumn grow;
So love and Beauty ftill that vifage grace;
Death cannot fright them from their wonted place.
Alive, the hand of crooked Age had marr'd
Thofe lovely features which cold Death has fpar'd. 10
    No wonder then he fped in love fo well,
When his high paffion he had breath to tell;

When that accomplifh'd foul, in this fair frame,
No bufinefs had but to perfuade that dame,
Whofe mutual love advanc'd the youth fo high,
That, but to heav'n, he could no higher fly.   16

XLVIII.

ON A

BREDE OF DIVERS COLOURS,

WOVEN BY FOUR LADIES.

Twice twenty flender virgin-fingers twine
This curious web, where all their fancies fhine.
As Natufe them, fo they this fhade have wrought,
Soft as their hands, and various as their thought.
Not Juno's bird, when, his fair train difpread,   5
He wooes the female to his painted bed;
No, not the bow, which fo adorns the fkies,
So glorious is, or boafts fo many dyes.   8

XLIX.

OF A WAR WITH SPAIN,

AND FIGHT AT SEA.

Now for fome ages had the pride of Spain
Made the fun fhine on half the world in vain,

While she bid War, to all that durst, supply
The place of those her cruelty made die.
Of Nature's bounty men forbore to taste, 5
And the best portion of the earth lay waste.
From the new world her silver and her gold
Came, like a tempest, to confound the old :
Feeding with these the brib'd Electors' hopes,
Alone she gives us Emperors and Popes : 10
With these accomplishing her vast designs,
Europe was shaken with her Indian mines.

When Britain, looking with a just disdain
Upon this gilded majesty of Spain,
And knowing well that empire must decline, 15
Whose chief support and sinews are of coin,
Our nation's solid virtue did oppose
To the rich troublers of the world's repose.

And now some months, encamping on the main,
Our naval army had besieged Spain : 20
They that the whole world's monarchy design'd,
Are to their ports by our bold fleet confin'd,
From whence our Red Cross they triumphant see,
Riding without a rival on the sea.

Others may use the ocean as their road, 25
Only the English make it their abode,
Whose ready sails with ev'ry wind can fly,
And make a cov'nant with th' inconstant sky :
Our oaks secure, as if they there took root,
We tread on billows with a steady foot. 30

Mean-while the Spaniards in America,
Near to the Line the fun approaching faw,
And hop'd their European coafts to find
Clear'd from our fhips by the autumnal wind :
Their huge capacious galleons ftuff'd with plate,   35
The lab'ring winds drive flowly tow'rds their fate.
Before St. Lucar they their guns difcharge,
To tell their joy, or to invite a barge :
This heard fome fhips of ours, (tho' out of view)
And, fwift as eagles, to the quarry flew ;   40
So heedlefs lambs, which for their mothers bleat,
Wake hungry lions, and become their meat.
· Arriv'd, they foon begin that tragic play,
And with their fmoky cannons banifh day :
Night, horror, flaughter, with confufion meets,   45
And in their fable arms embrace the fleets.
Thro' yielding planks the angry bullets fly,
And, of one wound, hundreds together die :
Born under diff'rent ftars one fate they have,
The fhip their coffin, and the fea their grave!   50
Bold were the men which on the ocean firft
Spread their new fails, when fhipwreck was the worft:
More danger now from man alone we find
Than from the rocks, the billows, or the wind.
They that had fail'd from near th' Antartic Pole,   55
Their treafure fafe, and all their veffels whole,
In fight of their dear country ruin'd be,
Without the guilt of either rock or fea !

What they would fpare our fiercer art deftroys,
Surpaffing ftorms in terror and in noife. 60
Once Jove from Ida did both hofts furvey,
And, when he pleas'd to thunder, part the fray;
Here heav'n in vain that kind retreat fhould found;
The louder cannon had the thunder drown'd.
Some we made prize; while others, burnt and rent, 65
With their rich lading to the bottom went:
Down finks at once (fo Fortune with us fports!)
The pay of armies, and the pride of courts.
Vain man! whofe rage buries as low that ftore
As avarice had digg'd for it before: 70
What earth, in her dark bowels, could not keep
From greedy hands, lies fafer in the deep,
Where Thetis kindly does from mortals hide
Thofe feeds of luxury, debate, and pride.

And now into her lap the richeft prize 75
Fell, with the nobleft of our enemies:
The Marquis *, (glad to fee the fire deftroy
Wealth that prevailing foes were to enjoy)
Out from his flaming fhip his children fent,
To perifh in a milder element; 80
Then laid him by his burning lady's fide,
And, fince he could not fave her, with her dy'd.
Spices and gums about them melting fry,
And, phœnix-like, in that rich neft they die:
Alive, in flames of equal love they burn'd, 85
And now together are to afhes turn'd;

* Of Bajadez.

Afhes! more worth than all their fun'ral coft,
Than the huge treafure which was with them loft.
Thefe dying lovers, and their floting fons,
Sufpend the fight, and filence all our guns: 90
Beauty and youth about to perifh, finds
Such noble pity in brave Englifh minds,
That (the rich fpoil forgot, their valour's prize)
All labour now to fave their enemies.
How frail our paffions! how foon changed are   95
Our wrath and fury to a friendly care!
They that but now for honour and for plate
Made the fea blufh with blood, refign their hate;
And, their young foes endeav'ring to retrieve,
With greater hazard than they fought they dive. 100
    With thefe returns victorious Montágu,
With laurels in his hand, and half Peru.
Let the brave generals divide that bough,
Our great Protector hath fuch wreaths enough :
His conqu'ring head has no more room for bays: 105
Then let it be as the glad nation prays;
Let the rich ore forthwith be melted down,
And the ftate fix'd by making him a crown :
With ermine clad, and purple, let him hold
A royal fceptre, made of Spanifh gold.   110

L.

UPON THE DEATH OF

THE LORD PROTECTOR.

WE muſt reſign! Heav'n his great ſoul does claim
In ſtorms, as loud as his immortal fame:
His dying groans, his laſt breath, ſhakes our iſle,
And trees uncut fall for his fun'ral pile;
About his palace their broad roots are toſt   5
Into the air.—So Romulus was loſt!
New Rome in ſuch a tempeſt miſs'd her king,
And from obeying fell to worſhipping.
On Oeta's top thus Hercules lay dead,
With ruin'd oaks and pines about him ſpread.   10
The poplar, too, whoſe bough he wont to wear
On his victorious head, lay proſtrate there.
Thoſe his laſt fury from the mountain rent:
Our dying hero from the continent
Raviſh'd whole towns; and forts from Spaniards reft, 15
As his laſt legacy to Britain left.
The ocean, which ſo long our hopes confin'd,
Could give no limits to his vaſter mind;
Our bounds' enlargement was his lateſt toil,
Nor hath he left us pris'ners to our iſle: 20
Under the tropic is our language ſpoke,
And part of Flanders hath receiv'd our yoke.

From civil broils he did us difengage,
Found nobler objects for our martial rage;
And, with wife conduct, to his country fhow'd   25
The ancient way of conquering abroad.

   Ungrateful then! if we no tears allow
To him that gave us peace and empire too.
Princes that fear'd him grieve, concern'd to fee
No pitch of glory from the grave is free.   30
Nature herfelf took notice of his death,
And, fighing, fwell'd the fea with fuch a breath,
That, to remoteft fhores her billows roll'd,
Th' approaching fate of their great ruler told.   34

LI.

ON ST. JAMES'S PARK,

AS LATELY IMPROVED BY HIS MAJESTY.

Of the firft Paradife there's nothing found;
Plants fet by Heav'n are vanifh'd, and the ground;
Yet the defcription lafts: who knows the fate
Of lines that fhall this paradife relate?

   Inftead of rivers rolling by the fide   5
Of Eden's garden, here flows in the tide:
The fea, which always ferv'd his empire, now
Pays tribute to our Prince's pleafure too.
Of famous cities we the founders know;
But rivers, old as feas, to which they go,   10

Are Nature's bounty : 'tis of more renown
To make a river than to build a town.
　For future shade, young trees upon the banks
Of the new stream appear in even ranks :
The voice of Orpheus, or Amphion's hand,　　15
In better order could not make them stand :
May they increase as fast, and spread their boughs,
As the high fame of their great owner grows!
May he live long enough to see them all
Dark shadows cast, and as his palace tall!　　20
Methinks I see the love that shall be made,
The lovers walking in that am'rous shade,
The gallants dancing by the river side;
They bathe in summer, and in winter slide.
Methinks I hear the music in the boats,　　·25
And the loud echo which returns the notes,
While over-head a flock of new-sprung fowl
Hangs in the air, and does the sun control,
Dark'ning the sky : they hover o'er, and shrowd
The wanton sailors with a feather'd cloud.　　30
Beneath a shoal of silver fishes glides,
And plays about the gilded barges' sides :
The ladies angling in the crystal lake,
Feast on the waters with the prey they take :
At once victorious with their lines and eyes,　　35
They make the fishes and the men their prize.
A thousand Cupids on the billows ride,
And sea-nymphs enter with the swelling tide;

M ij

From Thetis fent as fpies, to make report,
And tell the wonders of her fov'reign's court. 40
All that can, living, feed the greedy eye,
Or dead, the palate, here you may defcry :
The choiceft things that furnifh'd Noah's ark,
Or Peter's fheet, inhabiting this Park ;
All with a border of rich fruit-trees crown'd, 45
Whofe loaded branches hide the lofty mound.
Such various ways the fpacious alleys lead,
My doubtful Mufe knows not what path to tread.
Yonder, the harveft of cold months laid up,
Gives a frefh coolnefs to the royal cup : 50
There ice, like cryftal firm, and never loft,
Tempers hot July with December's froft ;
Winter's dark prifon, whence he cannot fly,
'Tho' the warm fpring, his enemy, draws nigh.
Strange! that extremes fhould thus preferve the fnow,
High on the Alps, or in deep caves below. 56
    Here a well-polifh'd Mall gives us the joy
To fee our Prince his matchlefs force employ ;
His manly pofture, and his graceful mien,
Vigour and youth, in all his motions feen ; 60
His fhape fo lovely, and his limbs fo ftrong,
Confirm our hopes we fhall obey him long.
No fooner has he touch'd the flying ball,
But 'tis already more than half the Mall ;
And fuch a fury from his arm has got, 65
As from a fmoking culv'rin it were fhot.

Near this my Muſe, what moſt delights her, ſees
A living gallery of aged trees ;
Bold ſons of Earth, that thruſt their arms ſo high,
As if once more they would invade the ſky.   70
In ſuch green palaces the firſt kings reign'd,
Slept in their ſhades, and angels entertain'd ;
With ſuch old counſellors they did adviſe,
And by frequenting ſacred groves grew wiſe.
Free from th' impediments of light and noiſe,   75
Man, thus retir'd, his nobler thoughts employs.
Here Charles contrives th' ord'ring of his ſtates,
Here he reſolves his neighb'ring princes' fates ;
What nation ſhall have peace, where war be made,
Determin'd is in this orac'lous ſhade ;   80
The world, from India to the frozen North,
Concern'd in what this ſolitude brings forth.
His fancy objects from his view receives ;
The proſpect thought and contemplation gives.
That ſeat of empire here ſalutes his eye,   85
To which three kingdoms do themſelves apply ;
The ſtructure by a prelate * rais'd, Whitehall,
Built with the fortune of Rome's Capitol :
Both, diſproportion'd to the preſent ſtate
Of their proud founders, were approv'd by Fate. 90
From hence he does that antique pile † behold,
Where royal heads receive the ſacred gold :

* Cardinal Wolſey.   † Weſtminſter-Abbey.

It gives them crowns, and does their ashes keep;
There made like gods, like mortals there they sleep:
Making the circle of their reign complete, 95
Those suns of Empire! where they rise they set.
When others fell, this standing did presage
The crown should triumph over pop'lar rage:
Hard by that House * where all our ills were shap'd
Th' auspicious temple stood, and yet escap'd. 100
So snow on Ætna does unmelted lie,
Whence rolling flames and scatter'd cinders fly;
The distant country in the ruin shares;
What falls from heav'n the burning mountain spares.
Next that capacious Hall † he sees, the room 105
Where the whole nation does for justice come;
Under whose large roof flourishes the gown,
And judges grave on high tribunals frown.
Here, like the people's pastor, he does go,
His flock subjected to his view below; 110
On which reflecting in his mighty mind,
No private passion does indulgence find:
The pleasures of his youth suspended are,
And made a sacrifice to public care.
Here, free from court compliances, he walks, 115
And with himself, his best adviser, talks,
How peaceful olives may his temples shade,
For mending laws, and for restoring trade:

.* House of Commons. † Westminster-Hall.

Or how his brows may be with laurel charg'd,
For nations conquer'd, and our bounds enlarg'd. 120
Of ancient prudence here he ruminates,
Of rising kingdoms and of falling states :
What ruling arts gave great Augustus fame,
And how Alcides purchas'd such a name.
His eyes, upon his native palace *,bent, 125
Close by, suggest a greater argument.
His thoughts rise higher, when he does reflect
On what the world may from that star expect
Which at his birth appear'd, to let us see
Day, for his sake, could with the night agree : 130
A prince on whom such diff'rent lights did smile,
Born the divided world to reconcile !
Whatever Heav'n, or high extracted blood
Could promise, or foretel, he will make good ;
Reform these nations, and improve them more
Than this fair Park, from what it was before. 136

LII.

Of the invasion and defeat

OF THE TURKS,

IN THE YEAR 1683.

The modern Nimród, with a safe delight
Pursuing beasts, that save themselves by flight,

* St. James's,

Grown proud, and weary of his wonted game,
Would Chriſtians chaſe, and ſacrifice to fame.

A prince with eunuchs and the ſofter ſex   5
Shut up ſo long, would warlike nations vex,
Provoke the German, and, neglecting Heav'n,
Forget the truce for which his oath was giv'n.

His Grand Viſier, preſuming to inveſt
The chief imperial city of the Weſt *,   10
With the firſt charge compell'd in haſte to riſe,
His treaſure, tents, and cannon, left a prize:
The ſtandard loſt, and janizaries ſlain,
Render the hopes he gave his maſter vain.
The flying Turks, that bring the tidings home,   15
Renew the mem'ry of his father's doom;
And his guard murmurs, that ſo often brings
Down from the throne their unſucceſsful kings.

The trembling Sultan's forc'd to expiate
His own ill conduct by another's fate :   20
The Grand Viſier, a tyrant, tho' a ſlave,
A fair example to his maſter gave;
He Baſſas' heads, to ſave his own, made fly,
And now, the Sultan to preſerve, muſt die.

The fatal bowſtring was not in his thought,   25
When, breaking truce, he ſo unjuſtly fought;
Made the world tremble with a num'rous hoſt,
And of undoubted victory did boaſt.

* Vienna.

Strangled he lies! yet seems to cry aloud,
To warn the mighty, and instruct the proud,   30
That of the great, neglecting to be just,
Heav'n in a moment makes an heap of dust.

The Turks so low, why should the Christians lose
Such an advantage of their barb'rous foes?
Neglect their present ruin to complete,   35
Before another Solyman they get?
Too late they would with shame, repenting, dread
That num'rous herd, by such a lion led:
He Rhodes and Buda from the Christians tore,
Which timely union might again restore.   40

But, sparing Turks, as if with rage possest,
The Christians perish, by themselves opprest:
Cities and provinces so dearly won,
That the victorious people are undone!

What angel shall descend to reconcile   45
The Christian states, and end their guilty toil?
A prince more fit from Heav'n we cannot ask
Than Britain's king, for such a glorious task;
His dreadful navy, and his lovely mind,
Gives him the fear and favour of mankind: 50
His warrant does the Christian faith defend;
On that relying, all their quarrels end.
The peace is sign'd, and Britain does obtain
What Rome had sought from her fierce sons in vain.

In battles won Fortune a part doth claim,   55
And soldiers have their portion in the fame:

In this fuccefsful union we find
Only the triumph of a worthy mind.
'Tis all accomplifh'd by his royal word,
Without unfheathing the deftrudive fword;   60
Without a tax upon his fubjedts laid,
Their peace difturb'd, their plenty, or their trade :
And what can they to fuch a Prince deny,
With whofe defires the greateft kings comply ?

   The arts of peace are not to him unknown;   65
This happy way he march'd into the throne;
And we owe more to Heav'n than to the fword,
The wifh'd return of fo benign a lord.

   Charles! by old Greece with a new freedom grac'd,
Above her antique heroes fhall be plac'd.   70
What Thefeus did, or Theban Hercules,
Holds no compare with this victorious peace ;
Which on the Turks fhall greater honour gain,
Than all their giants and their monfters flain :
Thofe are bold tales, in fabulous ages told,
This glorious act the living do behold.   76

LIII.

OF HER MAJESTY,

ON NEW-YEAR'S DAY, 1683.

WHAT revolutions in the world have been !
How are we chang'd fince we firft faw the Queen !

She, like the fun, does ftill the fame appear,
Bright as fhe was at her arrival here!
Time has commiffion mortals to impair,   5
But things celeftial is oblig'd to fpare.

   May ev'ry new year find her ftill the fame
In health and beauty as fhe hither came!
When Lords **and Commons**, with united **voice**,
Th' Infanta **nam'd**, approv'd the royal **choice** :   10
Firft of our queens whom not **the King** alone,
But the whole nation, lifted to the throne.

   With like confent, and like defert, was crown'd
The glorious Prince * that does the Turk confound.
Victorious both ! his conduct wins the day,   15
And her example chafes vice away :
Tho' louder fame attend the martial rage,
'Tis greater glory to reform the age.   18

LIV.

OF TEA,

COMMENDED BY HER **MAJESTY.**

Venus her myrtle, Phœbus has his bays ;
Tea both excels, which fhe vouchfafes to praife.
The beft of queens, and beft of herbs, we owe
To that bold nation which the way did fhow

---

* John Sobiefki, king of Poland.

To the fair region where the fun does rife,   5
Whofe rich productions we fo juftly prize.
The Mufe's friend, tea does our fancy aid,
Reprefs thofe vapours which the head invade,
And keeps that palace of the foul ferene,
Fit on her birth-day to falute the Queen.   10

LV.

OF HER ROYAL HIGHNESS,

Mother to the Prince of Orange: and of her portrait writ-
ten by the late Duchefs of York while fhe lived with her.

Heroic Nymph! in tempefts the fupport,
In peace the glory of the Britifh court!
Into whofe arms the church, the ftate, and all
That precious is, or facred here, did fall.
Ages to come, that fhall your bounty hear,   5
Will think you miftrefs of the Indies were:
'Tho' ftraiter bounds your fortune did confine,
In your large heart was found a wealthy mine:
Like the bleft oil, the widow's lafting feaft,
Your treafure, as you pour'd it out, increas'd.   10
While fome your beauty, fome your bounty fing,
Your native ifle does with your praifes ring:
But above all, a nymph * of your own train
Gives us your character in fuch a ftrain,

* Lady Anne Hyde.

3

As none but she, who in that court did dwell, 15
Could know such worth, or worth describe so well.
So while we mortals here at heav'n do guess,
And more our weakness than the place express,
Some angel, a domestic there, comes down,
And tells the wonders he hath seen and known. 20

LVI.

UPON HER MAJESTY'S *

NEW BUILDINGS AT SOMERSET-HOUSE.

GREAT Queen! that does our island bless
With princes and with palaces;
Treated so ill, chas'd from your throne,
Returning, you adorn the Town;
And with a brave revenge do show   5
Their glory went and came with you.

While Peace from hence and you were gone,
Your houses in that storm o'erthrown,
Those wounds which Civil rage did give,
At once you pardon and relieve.   10
Constant to England in your love,
As birds are to their wonted grove,
Tho' by rude hands their nests are spoil'd,
There the next spring again they build.

* Henrietta Maria, queen-dowager of K. Charles I.

Accusing some malignant star,   15
Not Britain, for that fatal war,
Your kindness banishes your fear,
Resolv'd to fix for ever here.

But what new mine this work supplies?
Can such a pile from ruin rise?   20
This, like the first creation, shows,
As if at your command it rose.

Frugality, and bounty too,
(Those diff'ring virtues) meet in you:
From a confin'd, well-manag'd store,   25
You both employ and feed the poor.

Let foreign princes vainly boast
The rude effects of pride and cost;
Of vaster fabrics, to which they
Contribute nothing but the pay: 30
This, by the Queen herself design'd,
Gives us a pattern of her mind:
The state and order does proclaim
The genius of that Royal Dame.
Each part with just proportion grac'd,   35
And all to such advantage plac'd,
That the fair view her window yields,
The town, the river, and the fields,
Ent'ring, beneath us we descry,
And wonder how we came so high.   40

She needs no weary steps ascend;
All seems before her feet to bend;

And here, as she was born, she lies,
High, without taking pains to rise. 44

LVII.

OF A TREE CUT IN PAPER.

Fair hand! that can on virgin-paper write,
Yet from the stain of ink preserve it white;
Whose travel o'er that silver field does show
Like track of leverets in morning snow.
Love's image thus in purest minds is wrought, 5
Without a spot or blemish to the thought.
Strange that your fingers should the pencil foil,
Without the help of colours or of oil!
For tho' a painter boughs and leaves can make,
'Tis you alone can make them bend and shake; 10
Whose breath salutes your new-created grove,
Like southern winds, and makes it gently move.
Orpheus could make the forest dance, but you
Can make the motion and the forest too. 14

LVIII.

OF THE LADY MARY,

PRINCESS OF ORANGE.

As once the lion honey gave,
Out of the strong such sweetness came;
A royal hero, no less brave,
Produc'd this sweet, this lovely dame.

N ij

To her the prince, that did oppose 5
Such mighty armies in the field,
And Holland from prevailing foes
Could so well free, himself does yield.

Not Belgia's fleet (his high command)
Which triumphs where the sun does rise, 10
Nor all the force he leads by land,
Could guard him from her conqu'ring eyes.

Orange with youth experience has;
In action young, in council old:
Orange is what Augustus was, 15
Brave, wary, provident, and bold.

On that fair tree which bears his name,
Blossoms and fruit at once are found:
In him we all admire the same,
His flow'ry youth with wisdom crown'd! 20

Empire and freedom reconcil'd
In Holland are by great Nassau:
Like those he sprung from just and mild,
To willing people he gives law.

Thrice-happy Pair! so near ally'd 25
In royal blood, and virtue too!
Now Love has you together ty'd,
May none this triple knot undo!

The church ſhall be the happy place
Where ſtreams which from the ſame ſource run, 30
Tho' divers lands a while they grace,
Unite again, and are made one.

A thouſand thanks the nation owes
To him that does protect us all,
For while he thus his niece beſtows, 35
About our iſle he builds a wall;

A wall! like that which Athens had,
By th' oracle's advice, of wood:
Had theirs been ſuch as Charles has made,
That mighty ſtate till now had ſtood. 40

LIX.

OF ENGLISH VERSE.

Poets may boaſt, as ſafely vain,
Their works ſhall with the world remain:
Both bound together live or die,
The verſes and the propheſy.

But who can hope his line ſhould long 5
Laſt in a daily changing tongue?
While they are new envy prevails,
And as that dies our language fails.

When architects have done their part,
The matter may betray their art : 10
Time, if we ufe ill-chofen ftone,
Soon brings a well-built palace down.

Poets that lafting marble feek,
Muft carve in Latin or in Greek :
We write in fand; our language grows, 15
And, like the tide, our work o'erflows.

Chaucer his fenfe can only boaft,
The glory of his numbers loft !
Years have defac'd his matchlefs ftrain,
And yet he did not fing in vain. 20

The beauties which adorn'd that age,
The fhining fubjects of his rage,
Hoping they fhould immortal prove,
Rewarded with fuccefs his love.

This was the gen'rous poet's fcope, 25
And all an Englifh pen can hope,
To make the fair approve his flame,
That can fo far extend their fame.

Verfe, thus defign'd, has no ill fate,
If it arrive but at the date 30
Of fading beauty; if it prove
But as long-liv'd as prefent love. 32

LX.

UPON THE EARL OF ROSCOMMON'S

Tranflation of Horace, De Arte Poeticá: and of the ufe of poetry.

Rome was not better by her Horace taught,
Than we are here to comprehend his thought:
The poet writ to noble Pifo there ;
A noble Pifo does inftruct us here;
Gives us a pattern in his flowing ftyle,   5
And with rich precepts does oblige our ifle :
Britain! whofe genius is in verfe exprefs'd,
Eold and fublime, but negligently drefs'd.

Horace will our fuperfluous branches prune,
Give us new rules, and fet our harp in tune;   10
Direct us how to back the winged horfe,
Favour his flight, and moderate his force.

Tho' poets may of infpiration boaft,
Their rage, ill govern'd, in the clouds is loft.
He that proportion'd wonders can difclofe,   15
At once his fancy and his judgment fhows.
Chafte moral writing we may learn from hence,
Neglect of which no wit can recompenfe.
The fountain which from Helicon proceeds,
That facred ftream! fhould never water weeds,   20
Nor make the crop of thorns and thiftles grow,
Which envy or perverted nature fow.

Well-founding verfes are the charm we ufe,
Heroic thoughts and virtue to infufe :
Things of deep fenfe we may in profe unfold,   25
But they move more in lofty numbers told.
By the loud trumpet, which our courage aids,
We learn that found, as well as fenfe, perfuades.
'The Mufes' friend, unto himfelf fevere,
With filent pity looks on all that err;   30
But where a brave, a public, action fhines,
That he rewards with his immortal lines.
Whether it be in council or in fight,
His country's honour is his chief delight;
Praife of great acts he fcatters as a feed   35
Which may the like in coming ages breed.
Here taught the fate of verfes, (always priz'd
With admiration, or as much defpis'd)
Men will be lefs indulgent to their faults,
And patience have to cultivate their thoughts.   40
Poets lofe half the praife they fhould have got,
Could it be known what they difcreetly blot,
Finding new words, that to the ravifh'd ear
May like the language of the gods appear,
Such as, of old, wife bards employ'd, to make   45
Unpolifh'd men their wild retreats forfake :
Law-giving heroes, fam'd for taming brutes,
And raifing cities with their charming lutes :
For rudeft minds with harmony were caught,
And civil life was by the Mufes taught.   50

So wand'ring bees would perish in the air,
Did not a sound, proportion'd to their ear,
Appease their rage, invite them to the hive,
Unite their force, and teach them how to thrive:
To rob the flow'rs, and to forbear the spoil,   55
Preserv'd in winter by their summer's toil;
They give us food which may with nectar vie,
And wax that does the absent sun supply.   58

LXI.

AD COMITEM MONUMETENSEM

DE BENTIVOGLIO SUO.

FLORIBUS Angligenis non hanc tibi necto corollam,
   Cùm satis indigenis te probet ipse Liber:
Per me Roma sciet tibi se debere, quòd Anglo
   Romanus didicit cultiùs ore loqui.
Ultima quæ tellus Aquilas duce Cæsare vidit,   5
   Candida Romulidum te duce scripta videt.
Consilio ut quondam Patriam nil juveris, esto!
   Sed studio cives ingenioque juvas.
Namque dolis liber hic instructus, et arte Batavâ,
   A Belga nobis ut caveamus, ait.   10
Horremus per te civilis dira furoris
   Vulnera; discordes Flandria quassa monet.
Hic discat miles pugnare, orare senator;
   Qui regnant, leni sceptra tenere manu.

Maĉte, Comes! virtute novâ : veſtri ordinis ingens 15
Ornamentum, ævi deliciæque tui!
Dum ſtertunt alii ſomno vinoque ſepulti,
Nobilis antiquo ſtemmate digna facis.   18

LXII.

ON THE DUKE OF MONMOUTH'S

Expedition into Scotland in the ſummer ſolſtice.

Swift as Jove's meſſenger, (the winged god *)
With ſword as potent as his charming rod,
He flew to execute the King's command,
And in a moment reach'd that northern land,
Where day contending with approaching night,   5
Aſſiſts the hero with continu'd light.

   On foes ſurpris'd and by no night conceal'd,
He might have ruſh'd, but noble pity held
His hand a while, and to their choice gave ſpace
Which they would prove, his valour or his grace. 10
This not well heard, his cannon louder ſpoke,
And then, like lightning, thro' that cloud he broke.
His fame, his conduct, and that martial look,
The guilty Scots with ſuch a terror ſtrook,
That to his courage they reſign the field,   15
Who to his bounty had refus'd to yield.
Glad that ſo little loyal blood it coſt,
He grieves ſo many Britons ſhould be loſt;

* Mercury.

Taking more pains, when he beheld them yield,
To fave the flyers than to win the field;   20
And at the Court his int'reft does employ,
That none, who 'fcap'd his fatal fword, fhould die.

  And now thefe rafh bold men their error find,
Not trufting one beyond his promife kind;
One! whofe great mind, fo bountiful and brave, 25
Had learn'd the art to conquer and to fave.

  In vulgar breafts no royal virtues dwell;
Such deeds as thefe his high extraction tell,
And give a fecret joy to him that reigns *,
To fee his blood triumph in Monmouth's veins; 30
To fee a leader whom he got and chofe,
Firm to his friends, and fatal to his foes.

  But feeing envy, like the fun, does beat,
With fcorching rays, on all that's high and great,
This, ill-requited Monmouth! is the bough 35
The Mufes fend to fhade thy conqu'ring brow.
Lampoons, like fquibs, may make a prefent blaze,
But time and thunder pay refpect to bays.
Achilles' arms dazzle our prefent view,
Kept by the Mufe as radiant and as new 40
As from the forge of Vulcan firft they came;
Thoufands of years are paft, and they the fame;
Such care fhe takes to pay defert with fame!
Than which no monarch, for his crown's defence,
Knows how to give a nobler recompenfe. 45

    * K. Charles II.

LXIII.

THE TRIPLE COMBAT.

WHEN thro' the world fair Mazarine had run,
Bright as her fellow-traveller the sun,
Hither at length the Roman Eagle flies,
As the last triumph of her conqu'ring eyes.
As heir to Julius, she may pretend   5
A second time to make this island bend;
But Portsmouth, springing from the ancient race
Of Britons, which the Saxon here did chase,
As they great Cæsar did oppose, makes head,
And does against this new invader lead.   10
That goodly nymph, the taller of the two,
Careless and fearless to the field does go.
Becoming blushes on the other wait,
And her young look excuses want of height.
Beauty gives courage; for she knows the day   15
Must not be won the Amazonian way.
Legions of Cupids to the battle come,
For Little Britain these, and those for Rome.
Dress'd to advantage, this illustrious pair
Arriv'd, for combat in the list appear.   20
What may the Fates design! for never yet
From distant regions two such beauties met.
Venus had been an equal friend to both,
And Vict'ry to declare herself seems loath:
          4

Over the camp, with doubtful wings, she flies,   25
Till Chloris shining in the field she spies.
The lovely Chloris well-attended came,
A thousand Graces waited on the dame:
Her matchless form made all the English glad,
And foreign beauties less assurance had :   30
Yet, like the Three on Ida's top, they all
Pretend alike, contesting for the ball:
Which to determine Love himself declin'd,
Lest the neglected should become less kind.
Such killing looks ! so thick the arrows fly !   35
That 'tis unsafe to be a stander-by.
Poets, approaching to describe the fight,
Are by their wounds instructed how to write.
They with less hazard might look on, and draw
The ruder combats in Alsatia;   40
And with that foil of violence and rage,
Set off the splendour of our Golden Age:
Where Love gives law, Beauty the sceptre sways,
And, uncompell'd, the happy world obeys.   44

LXIV.

OF AN ELEGY MADE BY MRS. WHARTON

ON THE EARL OF ROCHESTER.

THUS mourn the Muses, on the herse
Not strowing tears, but lasting verse,

Which so preserve the hero's name,
They make him live again in fame.

  Chloris, in lines so like his own,   5
Gives him so just and high renown,
That she th' afflicted world relieves,
And shews that still in her he lives:
Her wit as graceful, great, and good;
Ally'd in genius as in blood.   10

  His loss supply'd, now all our fears
Are, that the nymph should melt in tears.
Then, fairest Chloris! comfort take,
For his, your own, and for our sake,
Lest his fair soul, that lives in you,
Should from the world for ever go.   16

LXV.

UPON OUR LATE LOSS

OF THE DUKE OF CAMBRIDGE.

THE failing blossoms which a young plant bears,
Engage our hope for the succeeding years;
And hope is all which Art or Nature brings,
At the first trial, to accomplish things.
Mankind was first created an essay;   5
That ruder draught the deluge wash'd away.
How many ages pass'd, what blood and toil,
Before we made one kingdom of this isle!

How long in vain had Nature striv'd to frame
A perfect princefs ere her Highnefs came? 10
For joys fo great we muft with patience wait;
'Tis the fet price of happinefs complete.
As a firft fruit Heav'n claim'd that lovely boy;
The next fhall live, and be the nation's joy. 14

LXVI.

INSTRUCTIONS TO A PAINTER,

For the drawing of the pofture and progrefs of his Ma-
jefty's forces at fea, under the command of his Highnefs-
Royal; together with the battle and victory obtained
over the Dutch, June 3, 1665.

First draw the fea, that portion which between
The greater world and this of ours is feen:
Here place the Britifh, there the Holland fleet,
Vaft floting armies! both prepar'd to meet.
Draw the whole world, expecting who fhould reign, 5
After this combat, o'er the conquer'd main.
Make Heav'n concern'd, and an unufual ftar
Declare th' importance of th' approaching war.
Make the fea fhine with gallantry, and all
The Englifh youth flock to their Admiral, 10
The valiant Duke! whofe early deeds abroad,
Such rage in fight, and art in conduct fhow'd:

O ij

His bright sword now a dearer int'reft draws,
His brother's glory, and his country's cause.

   Let thy bold pencil hope and courage fpread 15
Thro' the whole navy, by that hero led:
Make all appear where fuch a Prince is by,
Refolv'd to conquer, or refolv'd to die.
With his extraction and his glorious mind,
Make the proud fails fwell more than with the wind:20
Preventing cannon, make his louder fame
Check the Batavians, and their fury tame.
So hungry wolves, tho' greedy of their prey,
Stop when they find a lion in their way.
Make him beftride the ocean, and mankind   25
Afk his confent to ufe the fea and wind.
While his tall fhips in the barr'd Channel ftand,
He grafps the Indies in his armed hand.

   Paint an Eaft-wind, and make it blow away
Th' excufe of Holland for their navy's ftay: 30
Make them look pale, and, the bold Prince to fhun,
Thro' the cold North and rocky regions run.
To find the coaft where morning firft appears,
By the dark pole the wary Belgian fteers;
Confeffing now, he dreads the Englifh more 35
Than all the dangers of a frozen fhore;
While from our arms, fecurity to find,
They fly fo far, they leave the day behind.
Defcribe their fleet abandoning the fea,
And all their merchants left a wealthy prey: 40

Our first success in war make Bacchus crown,
And half the vintage of the year our own.
The Dutch their wine, and all their brandy lose,
Disarm'd of that from which their courage grows;
While the glad English, to relieve their toil,   45
In healths to their great leader drink the spoil.

His high command to Afric's coast extend,
And make the Moors before the English bend:
Those barb'rous pirates willingly receive
Conditions such as we are pleas'd to give.   50
Deserted by the Dutch, let nations know
We can our own and their great bus'ness do;
False friends chastise, and common foes restrain,
Which worse than tempests did infest the main.
Within those Streights make Holland's Smyrna fleet
With a small squadron of the English meet;   56
Like falcons these, those like a num'rous flock
Of fowl, which scatter to avoid the shock.
There paint Confusion in a various shape;
Some sink, some yield; and, flying, some escape.   60
Europe and Africa, from either shore,
Spectators are, and hear our cannon roar;
While the divided world in this agree,
Men that fight so deserve to rule the sea.

But, nearer home, thy pencil use once more,   65
And place our navy by the Holland shore:
The world they compass'd while they fought with
But here already they resign the main :   [Spain,

Those greedy mariners, out of whose way
Diffusive Nature could no region lay,   70
At home, preserv'd from rocks and tempests, lie,
Compell'd, like others, in their beds to die.
Their single towns th' Iberian armies prest;
We all their provinces at once invest;
And in a month ruin their traffic more   75
Than that long war could in an age before.

But who can always on the billows lie?
The watry wilderness yields no supply.
Spreading our sails, to Harwich we resort,
And meet the beauties of the British court.   80
Th' illustrious Duchess, and her glorious train,
(Like Thetis with her nymphs) adorn the main.
The gazing sea-gods, since the Paphian Queen *
Sprung from among them, no such sight had seen.
Charm'd with the graces of a troop so fair,   85
Those deathless pow'rs for us themselves declare,
Resolv'd the aid of Neptune's court to bring,
And help the nation where such beauties spring:
The soldier here his wasted store supplies,
And takes new valour from the ladies' eyes.   90

Mean-while, like bees, when stormy winter's gone,
The Dutch (as if the sea were all their own)
Desert their ports, and, falling in their way,
Our Hamburg merchants are become their prey.
Thus flourish they, before the approaching fight, 95
As dying tapers give a blazing light.

* Venus.

To check their pride, our fleet half victuall'd goes,
Enough to serve us till we reach our foes;
Who now appear so numerous and bold,
The action worthy of our arms we hold.   100
A greater force than that which here we find
Ne'er pref's'd the ocean, nor employ'd the wind.
Restrain'd a while by the unwelcome night,
Th' impatient English scarce attend the light.
But now the morning, (heav'n severely clear!)   105
To the fierce work indulgent does appear;
And Phœbus lifts above the waves his light,
That he might see, and thus record, the fight.

As when loud winds from diff'rent quarters rush,
Vast clouds encount'ring one another crush;   110
With swelling sails so, from their sev'ral coasts,
Join the Batavian and the British hosts.
For a less prize, with less concern and rage,
The Roman fleets at Actium did engage;
They for the empire of the world they knew,   115
These for the Old contend, and for the New.
At the first shock, with blood and powder stain'd,
Nor heav'n nor sea their former face retain'd;
Fury and art produce effects so strange,
They trouble Nature, and her visage change.   120
Where burning ships the banish'd sun supply,
And no light shines but that by which men die,
There York appears! so prodigal is he
Of royal blood as ancient as the sea!

Which down to him, so many ages told,   125
Has thro' the veins of mighty monarchs roll'd!
The great Achilles march'd not to the field
Till Vulcan that impenetrable shield
And arms had wrought; yet there no bullets flew,
But shafts and darts which the weak Phrygians threw.
Our bolder hero on the deck does stand   131
Expos'd, the bulwark of his native land;
Defensive arms laid by as useless here,
Where massy balls the neighb'ring rocks do tear.
Some power unseen those princes does protect, 135
Who for their country thus themselves neglect.

  Against him first Opdam his squadron leads,
Proud of his late success against the Swedes,
Made by that action, and his high command,
Worthy to perish by a prince's hand.   140
The tall Batavian in a vast ship rides,
Bearing an army in her hollow sides;
Yet, not inclin'd the English ship to board,
More on his guns relies than on his sword;
From whence a fatal volley we receiv'd;   145
It miss'd the Duke, but his great heart it griev'd:
Three worthy persons* from his side it tore,
And dy'd his garment with their scatter'd gore.
Happy! to whom this glorious death arrives,
More to be valu'd than a thousand lives!   150
On such a theatre as this to die,
For such a cause, and such a witness by!

* Earl of Falmouth, Lord Muskerry, and Mr. Boyle.

Who would not thus a sacrifice be made,
To have his blood on such an altar laid?
The rest about him strook with horror stood,   155
To see their leader cover'd o'er with blood.
So trembled Jacob, when he thought the stains
Of his son's coat had issued from his veins.
He feels no wound but in his troubled thought;
Before for honour, now revenge he fought: 160
His friends in pieces torn, (the bitter news
Not brought by Fame) with his own eyes he views.
His mind at once reflecting on their youth,
Their worth, their love, their valour, and their truth,
The joys of court, their mothers, and their wives, 165
To follow him abandon'd,—and their lives!
He storms and shoots; but flying bullets now,
To execute his rage, appear too slow:
They miss, or sweep but common souls away;
For such a loss Opdam his life must pay.   170
Encouraging his men, he gives the word,
With fierce intent that hated ship to board,
And make the guilty Dutch, with his own arm,
Wait on his friends, while yet their blood is warm.
His winged vessel like an eagle shows,   175
When thro' the clouds to truss a swan she goes:
The Belgian ship unmov'd, like some huge rock
Inhabiting the sea, expects the shock:
From both the fleets men's eyes are bent this way,
Neglecting all the bus'ness of the day: 180

Bullets their flight, and guns their noise suspend;
The silent Ocean does th' event attend,
Which leader shall the doubtful vict'ry bless,
And give an earnest of the war's success,
When Heav'n itself, for England to declare,   185
Turns ship, and men, and tackle, into air.

   Their new commander from his charge is tost,
Which that young prince * had so unjustly lost,
Whose great progenitors, with better fate,
And better conduct, sway'd their infant state.   190
His flight tow'rds heav'n th' aspiring Belgian took,
But fell, like Phaeton, with thunder strook:
From vaster hopes than his he seem'd to fall,
That durst attempt the British Admiral:
From her broad sides a ruder flame is thrown   195
Than from the fiery chariot of the sun;
That bears the radiant ensign of the day,
And she the flag that governs in the sea.

   The Duke, (ill pleas'd that fire should thus prevent
The work which for his brighter sword he meant)200
Anger still burning in his valiant breast,
Goes to complete revenge upon the rest.
So on the guardless herd, their keeper slain,
Rushes a tiger in the Libyan plain:
The Dutch, accustom'd to the raging sea,   205
And in black storms the frowns of Heav'n to see,
Never met tempest which more urg'd their fears,
Than that which in the Prince's look appears.

    * Prince of Orange.

Fierce, goodly, young! Mars he resembles, when
Jove sends him down to scourge perfidious men; 210
Such as with foul ingratitude have paid
Both those that led, and those that gave them aid.
Where he gives on, disposing of their fates,
Terror and death on his loud cannon waits,
With which he pleads his brother's cause so well, 215
He shakes the throne to which he does appeal.
The sea with spoils his angry bullets strow,
Widows and orphans making as they go:
Before his ship fragments of vessels torn,
Flags, arms, and Belgian carcasses, are borne, 220
And his despairing foes, to flight inclin'd,
Spread all their canvass to invite the wind.
So the rude Boreas, where he lists to blow,
Makes clouds above, and billows fly below,
Beating the shore, and with a boist'rous rage 225
Does heav'n at once, and earth, and sea engage.
The Dutch, elsewhere, did thro' the watry field
Perform enough to have made others yield;
But English courage, growing as they fight,
In danger, noise, and slaughter, takes delight: 230
Their bloody task, unweary'd still, they ply,
Only restrain'd by death or victory.
Iron and lead, from earth's dark entrails torn,
Like show'rs of hail, from either side are borne:
So high the rage of wretched mortals goes, 235
Hurling their mother's bowels at their foes!

Ingenious to their ruin, ev'ry age
Improves the arts and instruments of rage.
Death-haft'ning ills Nature enough has sent,
And yet men still a thousand more invent! 240

But Bacchus now, which led the Belgians on,
So fierce at first, to favour us begun :
Brandy and wine, (their wonted friends) at length
Render them useless, and betray their strength.
So corn in fields, and in the garden flow'rs, 245
Revive and raise themselves with mod'rate show'rs;
But overcharg'd with never-ceasing rain,
Become too moist, and bend their heads again.
Their reeling ships on one another fall,
Without a foe, enough to ruin all. 250
Of this disorder, and the fav'ring wind,
The watchful English such advantage find,
Ships fraught with fire among the heap they throw,
And up the so-intangled Belgians blow.
The flame invades the powder-rooms, and then 255
Their guns shoot bullets, and their vessels men.
The scorch'd Batavians on the billows float,
Sent from their own, to pass in Charon's boat.

And now our Royal Admiral success
(With all the marks of victory) does bless: 260
The burning ships, the taken, and the slain,
Proclaim his triumph o'er the conquer'd main.
Nearer to Holland as their hasty flight
Carries the noise and tumult of the fight,

His cannons roar, forerunner of his fame, 265
Makes their Hague tremble, and their Amsterdam:
The British thunder does their houses rock,
And the Duke seems at ev'ry door to knock.
His dreadful streamer (like a comet's hair,
Threat'ning destruction) hastens their despair; 270
Makes them deplore their scatter'd fleet as lost,
And fear our present landing on their coast.

The trembling Dutch th' approaching Prince be-
As sheep a lion leaping tow'rds their fold : [hold
Those piles which serve them to repel the main, 275
They think too weak his fury to restrain.
" What wonders may not English valour work,
" Led by th' example of victorious York ?
" Or what defence against him can they make,
" Who at such distance does their country shake ? 280
" His fatal hand their bulwarks will o'erthrow,
" And let in both the ocean and the foe."
Thus cry the people;—and, their land to keep,
Allow our title to command the deep;
Blaming their States' ill conduct, to provoke 285
Those arms which freed them from the Spanish yoke.

Painter! excuse me, if I have a while
Forgot thy art, and us'd another style;
For tho' you draw arm'd heroes as they sit,
The task in battle does the Muses fit : 290
They in the dark confusion of a fight
Discover all, instruct us how to write;

And light and honour to brave actions yield,
Hid in the smoke and tumult of the field.
Ages to come shall know that leader's toil,   295
And his great name on whom the Muses smile:
Their dictates here let thy fam'd pencil trace,
And this relation with thy colours grace.

 Then draw the Parliament, the nobles met,
And our Great Monarch * high above them set : 300
Like young Augustus let his image be,
Triumphing for that victory at sea,
Where Egypt's Queen †, and Eastern Kings o'er-
Made the possession of the world his own. [thrown,
Last draw the Commons at his royal feet,   305
Pouring out treasure to supply his fleet :
They vow with lives and fortunes to maintain
Their King's eternal title to the main :
And with a present to the Duke, approve
His valour, conduct, and his country's love.   310

  * K. Charles II.   † Cleopatra.

LXVII.

A presage of the ruin

OF THE TURKISH EMPIRE:

presented to

HIS MAJESTY KING JAMES II.

on his birth-day.

Since James the Second grac'd the British throne,
Truce, well obferv'd, has been infring'd by none:
Chriftians to him their prefent union owe,
And late fuccefs againft the common foe;
While neighb'ring princes, loath to urge their fate, 5
Court his affiftance, and fufpend their hate.
So angry bulls the combat do forbear,
When from the wood a lion does appear.

   This happy day peace to our ifland fent,
As now he gives it to the Continent.   10
A prince more fit for fuch a glorious tafk
Than England's King, from Heav'n we cannot afk:
He (great and good!) proportion'd to the work,
Their ill-drawn fwords fhall turn againft the Turk.

   Such kings, like ftars with influence unconfin'd, 15
Shine with afpect propitious to mankind;
Favour the innocent, reprefs the bold,
And, while they flourifh, make an Age of Gold.

Bred in the camp, fam'd for his valour young ;
At sea successful, vigorous, and strong;   20
His fleet, his army, and his mighty mind,
Esteem and rev'rence thro' the world do find.
A prince with such advantages as these,
Where he persuades not, may command a peace.
Britain declaring for the juster side,   25
The most ambitious will forget their pride :
They that complain will their endeavours cease,
Advis'd by him, inclin'd to present peace,
Join to the Turk's destruction, and then bring
All their pretences to so just a king.   30
    If the successful troublers of mankind,
With laurel crown'd, so great applause do find,
Shall the vex'd world less honour yield to those
That stop their progress, and their rage oppose ?
Next to that Pow'r which does the ocean awe,   35
Is to set bounds, and give Ambition law.
    The British Monarch shall the glory have,
That famous Greece remains no longer slave;
That source of art and cultivated thought !
Which they to Rome, and Romans hither brought. 40
    The banish'd Muses shall no longer mourn,
But may with Liberty to Greece return :
Tho' slaves, (like birds that sing not in a cage)
They lost their genius and poetic rage ;
Homers again, and Pindars, may be found,   45
And his great actions with their numbers crown'd.

The Turk's vaſt empire does united ſtand :
Chriſtians, divided under the command
Of jarring princes, would be ſoon undone,
Did not this hero make their int'reſt one;   50
Peace to embrace, ruin the common foe,
Exalt the Croſs, and lay the Creſcent low.
    Thus may the Goſpel to the riſing ſun
Be ſpread, and flouriſh where it firſt begun ;
And this great day, (ſo juſtly honour'd here!)
Known to the Eaſt, and celebrated there.   56

> Haec ego longaevus cecini tibi, maxime regum !
> Auſus et ipſe manu juvenum tentare laborem."   Virg.

LXVIII.

THESE VERSES

were writ in the

TASSO OF HER ROYAL HIGHNESS,

Tasso knew how the fairer ſex to grace,
But in no one durſt all perfection place.
In her alone that owns this book is ſeen
Clorinda's ſpirit, and her lofty mien,
Sophronia's piety, Erminia's truth,   5
Armida's charms, her beauty, and her youth.
    Our Princeſs here, as in a glaſs, does dreſs
Her well-taught mind, and ev'ry grace expreſs.

P iij

More to our wonder than Rinaldo fought,
The hero's race excels the poet's thought. 10

LXIX.

THE BATTLE

OF THE

SUMMER-ISLANDS.

CANTO I.

What fruits they have, and how Heav'n smiles
Upon those late-discover'd isles!

Aid me, Bellona! while the dreadful fight
Betwixt a nation and two whales I write.
Seas stain'd with gore I sing, advent'rous toil!
And how these monsters did disarm an isle.

Bermuda, wall'd with rocks, who does not know? 5
That happy island where huge lemons grow,
And orange trees, which golden fruit do bear,
'Th' Hesperian garden boasts of none so fair;
Where shining pearl, and coral, many a pound,
On the rich shore, of ambergris is found. 10
The lofty cedar, which to heav'n aspires,
The prince of trees! is fuel for their fires:
The smoke by which their loaded spits do turn,
For incense might on sacred altars burn:
Their private roofs on od'rous timber borne, 15
Such as might palaces for kings adorn.

The sweet palmettos a new Bacchus yield,
With leaves as ample as the broadest shield,
Under the shadow of whose friendly boughs
They sit, carousing where their liquor grows.   20
Figs there unplanted thro' the fields do grow,
Such as fierce Cato did the Romans show,
With the rare fruit inviting them to spoil
Carthage, the mistress of so rich a soil.
The naked rocks are not unfruitful there,   25
But at some constant seasons, ev'ry year
Their barren tops with luscious food abound,
And with the eggs of various fowls are crown'd.
Tobacco is the worst of things, which they
To English landlords, as their tribute, pay.   30
Such is the mould that the blest tenant feeds
On precious fruits, and pays his rent in weeds.
With candy'd plantains and the juicy pine,
On choicest melons and sweet grapes they dine,
And with potatoes fat their wanton swine.   35
Nature these cates with such a lavish hand
Pours out among them, that our coarser land
Tastes of that bounty, and does cloth return,
Which not for warmth, but ornament, is worn:
For the kind spring, which but salutes us here,   40
Inhabits there, and courts them all the year.
Ripe fruits and blossoms on the same trees live;
At once they promise what at once they give.
So sweet the air, so moderate the clime,
None sickly lives, or dies before his time.   45

Heav'n fure has kept this fpot of earth uncurft,
To fhew how all things were created firft.
The tardy plants in our cold orchards plac'd,
Referve their fruit for the next age's tafte:
There a fmall grain in fome few months will be   50
A firm, a lofty, and a fpacious tree.
The palma-chrifti, and the fair papà,
Now but a feed, (preventing Nature's law)
In half the circle of the hafty year
Project a fhade, and lovely fruits do wear.   55
And as their trees, in our dull region fet,
But faintly grow, and no perfection get,
So in this northern tract our hoarfer throats
Utter unripe and ill-conftrained notes,
While the fupporter of the poets' ftyle,   60
Phœbus, on them eternally does fmile.
Oh! how I long my carelefs limbs to lay
Under the plantain's fhade, and all the day
With amorous airs my fancy entertain,
Invoke the Mufes, and improve my vein!   65
No paffion there in my free breaft fhould move,
None but the fweet and beft of paffions, love.
There while I fing, if gentle Love be by,
That tunes my lute, and winds the ftring fo high,
With the fweeet found of Sachariffa's name   70
I'll make the lift'ning favages grow tame.———
But while I do thefe pleafing dreams indite,
I am diverted from the promis'd fight.   73

CANTO II.

Of their alarm, and how their foes
Difcover'd were, this Canto fhows.

Tho' rocks fo high about this ifland rife,
That well they may the num'rous Turk defpife,
Yet is no human fate exempt from fear,
Which fhakes their hearts, while thro' the ifle they hear
A lafting noife, as horrid and as loud   5
As thunder makes before it breaks the cloud.
Three days they dread this murmur ere they know
From what blind caufe th' unwonted found may grow:
At length two monfters of unequal fize,
Hard by the fhore, a fifherman efpies;   10
Two mighty whales! which fwelling feas had toft,
And left them pris'ners on the rocky coaft;
One as a mountain vaft, and with her came
A cub, not much inferior to his dam.
Here in a pool, among the rocks engag'd,   15
They roar'd, like lions caught in toils, and rag'd.
The man knew what they were, who heretofore
Had feen the like lie murther'd on the fhore;
By the wild fury of fome tempeft caft,
The fate of fhips, and fhipwreck'd men, to tafte. 20
As carelefs dames, whom wine and fleep betray
To frantic dreams, their infants overlay;
So there, fometimes, the raging ocean fails,
And her own brood expofes; when the whales

Against sharp rocks, like reeling vessels quash'd,　25
Tho' huge as mountains, are in pieces dash'd:
Along the shore their dreadful limbs lie scatter'd,
Like hills with earthquakes shaken, torn, and shatter'd.
Hearts sure of brass they had who tempted first
Rude seas, that spare not what themselves have nurst.
The welcome news thro' all the nation spread,　31
To sudden joy and hope converts their dread:
What lately was their public terror, they
Behold with glad eyes as a certain prey;
Dispose already of th' untaken spoil,　35
And, as the purchase of their future toil,
These share the bones, and they divide the oil.
So was the huntsman by the bear opprest,
Whose hide he sold—before he caught the beast!

　They man their boats, and all their young men arm
With whatsoever may the monsters harm;　41
Pikes, halberts, spits, and darts that wound so far,
The tools of peace, and instruments of war.
Now was the time for vig'rous lads to show
What love or honour could invite them to:　45
A goodly theatre! where rocks are round
With rev'rend age and lovely lasses crown'd.
Such was the lake which held this dreadful pair
Within the bounds of noble Warwick's share:
Warwick's bold Earl! than which no title bears　50
A greater sound among our British peers;
And worthy he the mem'ry to renew,
The fate and honour to that title due,

Whose brave adventures have transferr'd his name,
And thro' the new world spread his growing fame.——
But how they fought, and what their valour gain'd,
Shall in another Canto be contain'd.   57

CANTO III.

The bloody fight, succefslefs toil,
And how the fishes fack'd the isle.

The boat which on the first assault did go,
Strook with a harping-ir'n the younger foe;
Who, when he felt his side so rudely gor'd,
Loud as the sea that nourish'd him he roar'd.
As a broad bream, to please some curious taste,   5
While yet alive, in boiling water cast,
Vex'd with unwonted heat he flings about
The scorching brass, and hurls the liquor out;
So with the barbed jav'lin stung, he raves,
And scourges with his tail the suff'ring waves.   10
Like Spenser's Talus with his iron flail,
He threatens ruin with his pond'rous tail;
Dissolving at one stroke the batter'd boat,
And down the men fall drenched in the moat;
With ev'ry fierce encounter they are forc'd   15
To quit their boats, and fare like men unhors'd.
 The bigger whale like some huge carrack lay,
Which wanteth sea-room with her foes to play:
Slowly she swims, and when, provok'd, she wou'd
Advance her tail, her head salutes the mud: 20

The fhallow water doth her force infringe,
And renders vain her tail's impetuous fwinge:
The fhining fteel her tender fides receive,
And there, like bees, they all their weapons leave.

This fees the cub, and does himfelf oppofe   25
Betwixt his cumber'd mother and her foes:
With defp'rate courage he receives her wounds,
And men and boats his active tail confounds.
Their forces join'd, the feas with billows fill,
And make a tempeft tho' the winds be ftill.   30
Now would the men with half their hoped prey
Be well content, and wifh this cub away:
Their wifh they have: he (to direct his dam
Unto the gap thro' which they thither came)
Before her fwims, and quits the hoftile lake,   35
A pris'ner there but for his mother's fake.
She, by the rocks compell'd to ftay behind,
Is by the vaftnefs of her bulk confin'd.
They fhout for joy! and now on her alone
Their fury falls, and all their darts are thrown.   40
Their lances fpent, one, bolder than the reft,
With his broad fword provok'd the fluggifh beaft:
Her oily fide devours both blade and haft,
And there his fteel the bold Bermudan left.
Courage the reft from his example take,   45
And now they change the colour of the lake:
Blood flows in rivers from her wounded fide,
As if they would prevent the tardy tide,

4

And raife the flood to that propitious height,
As might convey her from this fatal ftreight.   50
She fwims in blood, and blood does fpouting throw
To heav'n, that Heav'n men's cruelties might know.
Their fixed jav'lins in her fide fhe wears,
And on her back a grove of pikes appears;
You would have thought, had you the monfter feen 55
Thus dreft, fhe had another ifland been.
Roaring fhe tears the air with **fuch a noife,**
As well refembled the confpiring voice
Of routed armies, when **the** field is won,
To reach the ears of her efcaped fort.   60
He, tho' a league removed from the foe,
Haftes to her aid : the pious Trojan * fo,
Neglecting for Creufa's life his own,
Repeats the danger of the burning town.
The **men,** amazed, blufh **to** fee the feed   65
Of monfters human piety exceed.
Well proves this kindnefs, what the Grecian fung,
That **Love's** bright mother from the Ocean fprung.
Their courage droops, and, hopelefs now, they wifh
For compofition **with** th' unconquer'd fifh;   70
So fhe their weapons would reftore again,
Thro' **rocks** they'd hew her paffage to the main.
But how inftructed in each other's mind?
Or what commerce can men with monfters find?

* Aeneas.

Not daring to approach their wounded foe,   75
Whom her courageous son protected so,
They charge their musquets, and, with hot desire
Of fell revenge, renew the fight with fire;
Standing aloof, with lead they bruise the scales,
And tear the flesh of the incensed whales.   80
But no success their fierce endeavours found,
Nor this way could they give one fatal wound.
Now to their fort they are about to send
For the loud engines which their isle defend;
But what those pieces, fram'd to batter walls,   85
Would have effected on those mighty whales,
Great Neptune will not have us know, who sends
A tide so high that it relieves his friends.
And thus they parted with exchange of harms;
Much blood the monsters lost, and they their arms.   90

CONTENTS.

Q ij

Page

From the APOLLO PRESS,
    by the MARTINS,
      Sept. 8th, 1777.

END OF VOLUME FIRST.

www.ingramcontent.com/pod-product-compliance
Lightning Source LLC
Chambersburg PA
CBHW030601040726
47497CB00008B/2815